D0772542

Plantation Pageants

"BRER RABBIT . . . SOT UP AN' LAUGH" (page 243)

Plantation Pageants

BY

JOEL CHANDLER HARRIS

ILLUSTRATED BY E. BOYD SMITH

Short Story Index Reprint Series

BOOKS FOR LIBRARIES PRESS
FREEPORT, NEW YORK

First Published 1899
Reprinted 1970

STANDARD BOOK NUMBER:
8369-3396-6

LIBRARY OF CONGRESS CATALOG CARD NUMBER:
76-113667

PRINTED IN THE UNITED STATES OF AMERICA

CONTENTS

CHAP.		PAGE
I.	After the War	1
II.	A Visit from Aunt Minervy Ann	18
III.	A Strange Wagoner	39
IV.	Sweetest Susan's Strange Adventure	55
V.	A Visit to Billy Biscuit	73
VI.	Mr. Bobs and his Bubble	90
VII.	A Talk about Fox Hunting	109
VIII.	Old Scar-Face, the Red Fox, does some Bragging	123
IX.	Buster John sees Hodo	138
X.	Hodo gets his Blood up	156
XI.	Cawky, the Crow	173
XII.	The Story of Mr. Coon	191
XIII.	Flit, the Flying Squirrel	210
XIV.	The Diamond Mine	228

LIST OF ILLUSTRATIONS

PAGE

"Brer Rabbit . . . sot up an' laugh" (page 243) *Frontispiece*

Old June . . . thought she had lost her calf . 4

"Dey ain't no wagon dar!" 54

"Oh, what will mamma say?" 64

A wild beast of the forest, name unknown . 84

"He's going to show us something" 88

It was very wonderful 94

Drusilla turned and ran, and the children after her 104

"I am here, Son of Ben Ali" 122

Ready to disappear in the bushes 126

Hodo fawned on Buster John 144

Peeping from the sedge-field 154

Joe Maxwell, with Buster John . . . and Hodo . 158

The dog . . . had old Scar-Face in plain view . 168

"What is your name?" asked Buster John . 182

Cawky catching crows 188

Mr. Coon . . . examined them carefully . . 196

"I was wild with fear" 208

"Dey ain't no feathers on it; but 'tain't no bat" 212

"She leaned forward and looked at me" . . 222

very bad shape, so far as Buster John and Sweetest Susan were concerned. Something was wanting — the place was n't the same. The silence that fell upon everything, when the army clink-clanked out of hearing, was something terrible. The horses and mules stood under the big shed and shivered dumbly; and the cattle huddled together on the western side of the gin-house, for the wind was from the east, and blowing with a penetrating moisture that was more than cold.

There was no gossip among these animals that people think are dumb. They had been badly frightened by the hurly-burly that beset them; they might talk about it after a while when the sun shone out, or when the grass came; but meantime the east wind was blowing, and no matter how intelligent an animal may be, he can never tell what that wind will bring when it has begun to blow. Now the grass-eating animals know very well when a storm is coming. The flesh-eaters merely grow frisky and have a frolic; but the grass-eaters make for shelter, and if they have a home to go to, they go there; but the east wind — well, that is their problem, as it was Aaron's, only the son of Ben Ali never allowed it to blow on the back of his neck; so that when other people were going about complaining of rheumatism or neuralgia, or were in bed with pleurisy or pneumonia, the son of Ben Ali was usually on his feet and in fairly good health.

Well, on this remarkable day, the animals in the horse-lot and in the pasture were quiet and morose. They had been shaken up in the first place with their strange experiences, having been driven helter-skelter two or three miles from home in the wind and mist, and helter-skelter back again, with drums beating and bugles blowing, and nobody to explain it all. Old June, the milch cow, thought she had lost her calf, but after a while she felt it running along by her side, and it was standing under her now, a shivering, shaky, shaggy thing that looked more like a ba-ba-black-sheep than a respectable calf.

Anyhow, they all stood on the sheltered side of the gin-house, and were very quiet, as the steam rose from their backs and the fog issued from their nostrils. They were not in a playful mood, and there was nothing about them to interest Buster John and Sweetest Susan, when later in the day these young adventurers paid them a visit of inspection. Old June moaned at them in a familiar way, but that was all the welcome they received.

"I don't believe they 've been fed," said Sweetest Susan with a sigh.

"Why, of course not," exclaimed Buster John; "Aaron can't do everything."

"Where are Simon and Johnny Bapter and the rest?" the little girl asked.

Sure enough, where were they? Where were all the men and women, and the boys and girls, who used to make the negro quarters gay with laughter? Where was old Fountain? Yes, and where was Drusilla? This was the kind of day when there should be a fire blazing on the hearth of every cabin, if only to keep out the dampness; but smoke was coming out of only one chimney, and even that was not a free and friendly smoke. It was a thin, wavering ribbon of blue, hardly visible until the wind seized it and tore it to tatters.

"I don't know what you are going to do," said Sweetest Susan, "but I am going to find Drusilla. I have n't seen her since last night."

Sweetest Susan went toward the negro quarters, followed by Buster John, and as they went along

OLD JUNE . . . THOUGHT SHE HAD LOST HER CALF

they were even more and more impressed with the silence that had fallen over everything. On all rainy days, except this particular day, so far as they could remember, they could n't go within a quarter of a mile of the quarters without hearing singing and loud laughter, or the sound of negroes scuffling and wrestling. But now the whole place seemed to be deserted. Big Sal's cabin was the first they came to. The door was open, and they entered. For a moment the interior was so dark that they saw nothing, but presently they could see Big Sal sitting on the floor, carding out her gray hair. Usually she wore it in wraps, but they were now untwisted, and, as she carded them out, they stood at right angles to her head, and gave her a very wild and ferocious appearance.

She neither turned nor paused in the carding when the children stepped somewhat timidly in the door. People said she was sullen; but she was very sensitive and tender-hearted, and always famishing for some one to love. The negroes thought she was both cruel and suspicious, and Buster John and Sweetest Susan were somewhat doubtful about her. For a woman of sixty years, who had known hard work, and trouble with it, she was well preserved.

"Aunt Big Sal," said Sweetest Susan, "where is everybody?"

"Gone, honey, de Lord knows whar; gone, honey, de Lord knows how."

She turned as she spoke, and her hair bristling out gave her countenance such a wild aspect that the children involuntarily shrank back. They had never seen her with her hair down before.

She raised her hands. "Be afeard er any an' ev'ybody, honey, but don't be afeard er me! Dodge frum one an' all, but don't dodge frum me. Not frum me! No, my Lord!"

"Are they all gone?" asked Buster John.

"Mighty nigh all, honey; mighty nigh all un um. Dem what went wuz big fools, an' dem what stayed may be bigger ones, fer all I know. I 'd 'a' been gone myse'f, but I went 'roun' yander in de grave-yard, whar dey put dat cripple chile, an' sump'in helt me. I could n't go 'way an' leave 'im." She was speaking of Little Crotchett, who had been dead and buried these many long years.

"Why did they go?" inquired Sweetest Susan.

"Huntin' freedom," responded Big Sal. "Yes, Lord, huntin' freedom! I hope dey 'll fin' it; dat I does."

"Grandfather says all the negroes are free now," said Sweetest Susan.

"Did he say dat? Did he say dat wid his own mouf? Well, I thank my stars! I'm free, den! Me an' all de balance!"

"So Grandfather says," remarked Buster John.

"Well," said Big Sal, "ef I'm free, I better get up frum here an' go ter work. What does Marster want us ter do? I'm gwine up dar an' ax 'im."

The children went to the other cabins and found them empty, but in Jemimy's house they found Drusilla crying. You may imagine Sweetest Susan's grief when she made this discovery. Drusilla was ready with her tale of woe.

"Mammy walloped me kaze I won't go off wid de balance un um," sobbed Drusilla. "She say ef I stay here she got ter stay. I tell her I'll do anything but dat; I'll tell lies, I'll steal, but I won't go off frum here; dey got to kill me dead an' tote me. An' den mammy walloped me."

"You need n't ter b'lieve a word er dat!" cried Jemimy, who came in at that moment. "I tol' dat gal it would be better for we all ter go ef we wanter be free sho 'nuff, an' wid dat she fell on de flo' and 'gun to waller an' holler, tell I 'bleege to paddle 'er. I don't wanter go no wuss 'n she do, but dey say dat if we don't go 'way from whar we b'long at, we never is ter be free. Dat what de niggers on de nex' plantation say. I wuz born here, an' ef dis ain't my home, I dunner whar in de roun' worl' I got any."

There was a break in Jemimy's voice as she said this. Buster John paid no attention to it; but Sweetest Susan went close to her and leaned against her, and the negro woman put an arm around the child. It was as if a tramp steamer had thrown out an anchor within sight of the lights of home.

"Who cooked breakfast this morning?" asked Sweetest Susan.

"Me," replied Jemimy. "I know'd somebody had ter cook."

"I thought so," said the child. "The biscuits were mighty good."

It was some time before Jemimy said anything. She rose and pushed the child from her, remarking: "I dunner what come over me, but ef I set here wid my arm 'roun' you, an' you talkin' dat away, I 'll be boo-hooin' 'fo' I know myse'f. Git up frum dar, Drusilla, 'fo' I break yo' neck!"

Before Drusilla could make any preparation to rise, there came a loud rap on the door-facing.

"Nobody but old Fountain," said the new-comer; "old Fountain, as muddy as a hog, and harmless as a dove."

Harmless or not, he was certainly muddy. As he came in, the legs of his pantaloons, rubbing together, sounded as if they were made of leather. His coat was full of red mud, and mud was on his hat and in his hair.

"Whar is you been?" asked Jemimy.

"Fur enough ter go no furder," responded old Fountain, shaking his head. "I went a-huntin' freedom. De kin' I foun' will las' me a whet; I promise you dat."

"You don 't tell me!" exclaimed Jemimy.

"I does," said Fountain, "an' I could tell yo' lots mo' dan dat ef I had time. Dey sot me ter work liftin' waggin wheels out er de quagmire, an' den a driver rap-jacketed me wid his whip — well, you see me here, don't you? An' ef we 're bofe alive, you 'll see me here ter-morrow an' de day after."

"An' dey wa'n't no freedom dar?" questioned Jemimy. She spoke under her breath, as if afraid to hear the answer.

"I won't say dat," replied Fountain. "Fer dem dat like de kin', 'twuz dar. Some mought like de change, but not me. I bless God fer what I seed, but I seed 'nuff. I went, an' I come."

"Why n't you stop an' wash de mud off in de branch?" Jemimy asked presently.

"No, not me," Fountain replied, still shaking his head. "Ter stop wuz ter stay. I know'd dey wuz a branch at home; an' mo' dan dat, a spring. De idee wuz ter hurry back an' see ef de natchel groun' had been left!"

"I b'lieve you!" sighed Jemimy. "I come mighty nigh gwine myself."

"You 'd 'a' been sorry!" exclaimed Fountain; "you 'd 'a' been sorry plum ter yo' dyin' day. You see me?" Jemimy nodded her head. "Well, I been dar. I been right wid um. You can't call it freedom atter you wade thoo dat mud an' water."

Some one else came to the door. "All eyes open!" cried the newcomer. It was the refrain of hide-and-seek, and the children laughed when they heard it. They knew the voice of Johnny Bapter. "All eyes open!" he persisted. "I 'm It. Ten, ten, double-ten, forty-five, fifteen! All eyes open?"

With that Johnny Bapter walked in. He was a thin-looking negro, with a long face, and a mouth that was always laughing. He would have been very tall, but he stooped a trifle, and there was a limp to his walk. One of his feet dragged slightly, but he was nimble as a squirrel for all that. His clothes were wet, but not muddy. He hit his wool hat against the side of the chimney, and it left its damp print. He looked at the children and pointed to the wet place. "I tuck its dagarrytype," he said. Johnny Bapter had once lived in town, and his adventures there, as he made them out, would have filled a book; and, at times, they were interesting.

"I hope you-all been well," said Johnny Bapter; "I 'm sorter middlin' peart myse'f."

"Whar you been?" asked Jemimy.

"Kinder see-sawin' 'roun', follerin' de ban's, an' keepin' off de boogers."

"You did n't go wid um?"

"No 'm; not me; I seed dey had plenty comp'ny. Mo' dan dat, I seed um hit ol' man Fountain dar a whack er two, an' I 'lowed dat ez dey done come dis fur an' nobody ain't hurt um, maybe dey 'd git 'long all right. Dey ain't offer me no money fer ter go 'long and take keer un um. I wuz over dar at de camps las' night, an' I see niggers fightin' over scraps an' I hear chillun cryin' fer bread after de lights done put out. So wid me, it wuz Howdy, and good-by, and I wish you mighty well. What mo' can a nigger do?"

"Dat 's so," sighed Jemimy. "Whar de balance er our folks?"

"Oh, dey 'll come back in de due time," said Johnny Bapter laughing. "One 'll turn back at one branch, an' one at anudder; an' dem what don't turn back at de branch will sho turn back at de river. Dey 'll all be home 'fo' de week 's out."

Buster John and Sweetest Susan listened to all this, but said nothing. Their minds hardly grasped the problem with which the negroes were wrestling. They were free, if they went away. Would they be free if they stayed? It was a very serious matter.

"What dey gwine do when dey come back?" Jemimy asked.

"Work," exclaimed Fountain. "Yes, Lord! work frum sun-up ter sun-down."

"An' dey free too?" suggested Jemimy. She wanted to get at the bottom of the matter.

Johnny Bapter laughed. "Why, in town whar I stayed, de free white folks work harder dan niggers. De clerks in de sto' come rushin' ter dinner, an' dey 'd fling der hats on a cheer, snatch a mouffle er vittles, an' rush out wuss 'n ef de overseer wuz hollerin' at um."

"Is dat so?" replied Jemimy.

"Des like I tell you," said Johnny Bapter.

"I 've looked at it up an' down," remarked Fountain, "an' it 's dis away — de man what eats honest bread is got to work. Dat what de Bible say; maybe not in dem words."

"It sho is so," remarked Johnny Bapter laughing. "I 'll work all day an' half de night, but I don' wanter hear no bugles blow."

Just then Big Sal, who had fixed up her hair, and was quite presentable, having put on her Sunday clothes, came into the cabin and stood over against the fireplace.

"Wuz dey many er we-all wid dem ar white folks?" she asked.

"Well 'um, I should sesso!" exclaimed Fountain; "too many, lots too many; more dan day 'll find rashuns fur, ef I ain't mighty much mistaken."

"What dey all gwine 'long fer?" asked Big Sal.

"Dey er feared ef dey stay at home dey won't be free. Now, how 'bout dat?" suggested Fountain.

"Why, grandfather says the negroes are free, whether they go or stay," said Buster John. "Grandfather says he is mighty glad the black folks across the creek are free."

"Dey been prayin' fer it 'long 'nuff," remarked Big Sal.

"We-all is free 'nuff," said Johnny Bapter, "but who gwine ter feed us?"

"Dat is so; dat is sho one way fer ter look at it," exclaimed Fountain uneasily.

"Well," exclaimed Jemimy, "I know one thing an' dat ain't two; I'd ruther starve right here, whar I been born at, dan starve way off in de woods whar nobody don't know me."

A shadow darkened the door, and there stood Aaron, his right hand raised.

"Well, well! What's all this? Everything to do, and nobody to do it!" He whistled low under his breath. "Horses and mules to feed, hogs to call, sheep to salt, calves to take away from the cows. Well, well! I hear calls for meal, meat, syrup."

"Hit 's a fac'," assented Fountain.

"You hear my min' workin," said Johnny Bapter. "Make me a hoss out'n meal, meat an' syrup, and I 'll eat 'im up 'fo' yo' eyes."

He rose, stretched himself, let one side of his face drop with affected sorrow, while the other side was laughing, winked at the children, and darted out into the mist and rain. Presently the children heard him calling, first the hogs, and then the sheep.

Aaron and Fountain followed more sedately, and in the course of half an hour the horses and mules could be heard tearing the fodder from the racks and munching the ears of corn. By dinner time, according to Aaron's report, there was but one hand missing from the place; and as he had been hired from the Myrick estate, it was not expected that he would take up his abode on the Abercrombie plantation.

The fact that all the men, women, and children came back after taking a short holiday would have been somewhat puzzling to the children's father, if he had been at home; he had imbibed some of the modern ideas of business. It would cost something to clothe and feed them during the winter months, and all this would be clear loss, since their labor would not be profitable until the planting season began. But there was no problem in it for the White-Haired Master, the children's grandfather. He looked forward to a period of chaos and confusion, when labor would be hard to secure. Besides, as he said, the negroes had helped to make the ample supply of provisions with which the smokehouse was stocked, and they were entitled to a share of it, especially if they were willing to remain. Moreover, nearly all were born at the place and knew no other home.

And the plantation seemed to be very lucky in all respects. There were twenty bales of cotton stored under the gin-house shed, and before Christmas day they were sold at an average of $250 apiece — cotton was high directly after the war. This put $5000 in greenbacks in the plantation treasury; and in that, as in other things, the Abercrombie place was more fortunate than any of the other plantations for miles and miles around.

But Buster John and Sweetest Susan did n't think so. Everybody was so busy — even Johnny Bapter, who used to laugh and loaf every chance he had — that the children were driven back upon themselves. They could talk to the animals on the place, but that sort of thing ceases to be interesting when you have nothing else to do. They made signals to Mrs. Meadows, and waited patiently about the spring, hoping to catch a glimpse of Little Mr. Thimblefinger. But all to no purpose. Buster John was disgusted, and said so; but Sweetest Susan had clearer ideas about the matter.

"What can you expect?" she asked. "If you were Mr. Thimblefinger, what would you have done when you saw that great crowd of men and wagons, and heard the drums and the brass horns? Why, you would n't show your head in a year. And as for Mrs. Meadows, one of the soldiers let his horse drink from the spring. What do you suppose Mrs. Meadows thought when she saw that kind of a shadow staring at her through the water?"

"Well, grandfather says war is the worst thing that ever happened in the world," said Buster John, "and I reckon it is."

II.

A VISIT FROM AUNT MINERVY ANN.

THE cold and gloomy weather brought by the east wind soon cleared away, and the sun shone out bright and clear, with a warm breeze from the south, — a breeze that brought out the violets in great profusion. Still, the place was not the same. The negroes ceased their songs, except Johnny Bapter, and even he did n't sing as loudly or as constantly as he used to do. And they ceased to wrestle and play at night. It seemed that they had problems to consider. They were not sure of their position; they had nobody to advise them. They might have asked advice on the subject, but freedom appeared to add to their shyness, and they refrained from asking for any information or advice. Just why this should be so, nobody has ever discovered to this day. Some of the less fortunate found strangers to advise with them and to make them promises that were never to be redeemed; but on the Abercrombie place the negroes worked in the dark, as the saying is, except for such counsel as the strong common sense of Aaron was able to give them. They had the idea that, having been made the object of what seemed to be a special interposition of Providence, they were to be sustained and maintained in the same way.

This accounted for the fact that the negroes on most of the plantations left home and flocked to the towns and cities, where they became the charge of the Freedmen's Bureau, an institution that did a great deal of good, as well as a great deal of harm: a great deal of good, because in many cases it prevented actual starvation; and a great deal of harm, because it left the impression on the minds of the negroes that they were to be supported by the government whether they worked or not.

But the youngsters who read will say, "What of that?" and cry, "Get along with your pokey old story, if you have any to tell!" And it is good advice, too; but when you are writing about a certain period, you want to have something more than the local color; you want to get at the temper, the attitude, the disposition of the people you are writing about; so that when the youngsters of to-day get a little older they will be able to say, "There 's a great deal of foolishness in that old book, and some history, too," as if their youngsters will care any more for history than they did.

Well, anyhow, the sun was shining brightly and the air was warm. The tools and instruments of war were following the courses of the streams that plough seaward, and nature on the Abercrombie place had forgotten all about them. But, let the sun shine ever so brightly, the children failed to find Mr. Thimblefinger, and no message came from Mrs. Meadows. They were patient enough, too. Every day, sometimes in the morning and sometimes in the afternoon, they wandered down to the spring and sat on a dry Bermuda embankment, where they could watch developments.

It was noticed that Drusilla never joined in the regrets that Buster John and Sweetest Susan expressed, when day after day passed and no Mr. Thimblefinger came.

"I don't believe you care whether he comes or not," cried Sweetest Susan.

Drusilla shook her head. "I 'd keer mightily

ef he did come," she said frankly. "I done been down dar long wid 'im once, and goodness knows I don't wanter resk it no mo'. Hit seem lak a skeery dream den, an' I don't want no sech dream ter come ter me no mo'. When folks git so dat water won't wet um, dey better be gwine off ter some yuther country."

"What 's the matter with you?" asked Buster John brusquely.

"You better ax what de matter wid you-all," exclaimed Drusilla. "Dey ain't nothin' 't all de matter wid me. But I 'll say dis, when you-all see dat ar Mr. Fimblethinger — ever what his name is — you won't see me. Dat 's what! I 'll set here wid you twel he pop outen de water, and den I 'll pop 'way fum here. Ef I 'm free, dat 's whar my freedom will shine out."

"Well, you went once," remonstrated Sweetest Susan.

"Dat kinder doin's is like chills an' fever; you may have um once, but you don't want um twice."

"She 'll go," said Buster John.

Drusilla laughed. "I sholy will — 'way fum here. I don't see what you-all wanter fool wid dat kinder doin's fer. I'd lots druther see you-all jabberin' wid de jay-birds. Dat's bad nuff, but it's better 'n reskin' yo' life down und' dat spring. Kaze when you go down dar, dey ain't no tellin' ef you gwine ter come back 'live. En spozen 't wuz ter cave in on you — yo' pa, and yo' ma, and yo' grandpa would be gwine 'roun' here plum 'stracted, an' dey never would see hair ner hide er you while de worl' stan's. Uh-uh! I been down dar once, and dat uz twice too many. Dat ar Mr. Fimblefinger kin pop up and pop down, but I ain't gwine ter pop wid 'im, not less 'n I take leave er my senses."

The children could n't help but laugh at Drusilla's earnestness, and they laughed with a better heart because they knew that if they should have another opportunity to visit the country next door to the world, Drusilla would not allow them to go alone. But the opportunity never came, and they not only ceased to expect it, but presently fell in with other adventures that were quite as curious and as interesting, all of which are to be chronicled, however clumsily, in the pages to follow.

Meanwhile, one afternoon when the sun was preparing to go to bed, and when the children were still expecting little Mr. Thimblefinger, they heard a voice calling from the big road, which was not far away from the spring: —

"Heyo dar, folks! Will yo' dogs bite?" The voice was that of a negro woman. She was driving a small steer to a wagon, but had left the vehicle on the side of the road and had come over the stile. She was tall, and appeared to be about forty years old. She had a countenance that could smile, but its aspect was now serious, and her eye was bright and keen.

"You-all oughter know me!" she cried, as she came up. "Dat is, ef eve'ything ain't been run outen yo' heads by de war-hosses and de war-whoopers."

"I know you!" cried Sweetest Susan; "it's Aunt Minervy Ann Perdue."

"De same," assented Aunt Minervy Ann. "An' not de same nuther. Kaze, I tell you, honies, dey's a mighty change whar I live at. You ain't seen Mars Tumlin Perdue go 'long by de road, is you? Well, it's jest like 'im ter be stoppin' some'rs on de road talkin' politics. I b'lieve dat man ud stop on de road and talk politics ef he knowed eve'y minit wuz ter be de nex'.

I hear tell," Aunt Minervy went on, "dat de Yankees sweep over you-all's place an' never tuck off a blessed thing."

The children confirmed this by saying that the troops not only had not carried anything off, but had driven two mules into the lot that didn't belong there. "It would be funny," Buster John said, "if the two mules should turn out to belong to Major Perdue." Anyhow, some of the negroes had said the mules belonged to the major.

"You see dat lil steer out dar," exclaimed Aunt Minervy Ann, "'tain't much more dan a yearlin'; well, dat ar steer is de onliest four-footed creetur dat dey lef' at Perdue's; an' dey would n't 'a' lef' him ef I had n't a driv' 'im in my house an' kep' 'im in dar whiles dem people wuz rumagin' 'roun' an' trompin' by. Dey shot de chickens yit, an' de turkeys, an' even down ter de goslin's; an' dey fair stripped de smoke-'ouse an' de sto'-room."

"That 's mighty funny," remarked Buster John.

"It may seem like hit 's funny to you-all, honey," said Aunt Minervy Ann, "but 'tain't funny up dar whar we-all live at. Dey would n't 'a' done so bad ef it had n't 'a' been fer Mars Tumlin. He went out, he did, time dey come in de yard, an' he cuss'd um an' sass'd um des ez long ez dey wuz a'er one un um in sight. I tried to make signs fer ter make 'im hush, but, shoo! his dander wuz up, and you des ez well make signs at a gate-post. He say he gwine ter move ter town; an' when I ax 'im what we gwine live on, he 'low dat we can starve lots better in town dan we kin in de country; an' I spec' dat 's so, kaze we won't be so lonesome. Dey ain't a livin' soul on dat place but me and Mars Tumlin, an' yo' cousin Vallie an' Hamp. All de niggers done gone, kaze when dey come an' ax Mars Tumlin what dey mus' do, he bein' mad, 'lowed dey could all go to de ol' Boy, and be janged. He say he comin' over here fer ter borry sump'n ter eat; and he better be comin', too, fer de day 'll be gone fo' you know it."

"Yonder he is now," said Sweetest Susan. The children were well acquainted with Major Perdue. He was not only kin to them in some remote way, but he was very jolly company when in the humor — and this was pretty much all the time; for although the major had a temper which he took small pains to control, it was only on rare occasions that he displayed it. He was in a fine humor now, for he came forward laughing and gave the children each a hearty smack.

"Minervy Ann," said the major, "I thought I told you to curry that horse and plait his mane before you hitched him to the buggy."

"You did tell me dat," replied Minervy Ann; "an' I tol' you dat ef you 'd get some hot water an' soap, an' wash de horn off his haid, I 'd plait bofe mane an' tail."

"I clean forgot it," the major declared. "Well, you stay here and talk to these chaps, and I 'll call on Cousin Abercrombie and see if I can't beg or borrow a few rations. When I want you I 'll call you, and then you can drive your carriage in at the side gate there."

Aunt Minervy Ann looked after the major and laughed. "I hope ter goodness," she said, as she sat down by the children — "I hope ter goodness dat he won't say he want de vittles cooked. Kaze ef he done dat, it 'd put me in min' er dat ol' tale my mammy useter tell me."

"What tale was that?" Sweetest Susan asked.

"Oh! you-all done hear tell un it mo' times dan your been ter chu'ch. You ain't never had ol' Remus to tell it; but dar is dat ol' A'on, an' ol' Fountain, an' Big Sal — what dey been doin' all dis time ef dey ain't never tol' you dat tale? Ef dey ain't got sense 'nuff fer ter tell you all de tales dey is gwine, you better sic de dogs on um an' run um off de place — ef you got any dogs lef'."

"Well, they don't tell us any tales," said Buster John truly enough. "Old Aunt Free Polly used to tell us some; but that 's been so long ago that we 've forgotten them. You ought not to have said anything about a tale if you did n't want to tell it."

Aunt Minervy Ann looked at the child and laughed. "Heyo, here!" she exclaimed. "Ef dey 's gwine ter be any swellin' up an' gittin' mad, I 'll tell de tale, and git 'way fum here des quick ez I kin. I ain't come ter dis place fer ter git in no fuss."

The children composed themselves comfortably on the dead grass, and Aunt Minervy Ann told the story of

BRER RABBIT AND THE GOOBERS.

"Way back yander," said Aunt Minervy Ann, retying her head handkerchief, "de times wid de creeturs wuz mighty much like dey is wid folks now, speshually we-all up dar at de Perdue plantation. Dey wuz hard times. I disremember whedder dey had been a war and de army swep' 'long, or whedder dey wuz a dry drouth. Dey ain't much diffunce when craps fail.

"Well, anyhow, de times wuz mighty hard. Vittles wuz skacer dan hen's tushes, an' dem what had it, hid it. An' ef dey ain't hide it, dey stayed mighty close by it. Ol' Brer Rabbit wuz in jest ez bad fix ez any un um, ef not wuss. Slick ez he wuz, he wa'n't slick nuff fer ter git sump'n ter eat whar dey wa'n't none. De calamus patch gun out, all de saplin's had been barked higher up dan Brer Rabbit kin reach, de tater patches wuz empty, an' de pea vines wuz dry nuff fer ter ketch fire widout any he'p.

"So dar 'twuz. Like de common run er po' white folks, Brer Rabbit had a big fam'ly. De young uns wuz constant a-cryin' 'Daddy! Daddy! fetch me sump'n ter eat!' An' ol' Mis' Rabbit wuz dribblin' at de mouf, she wuz dat hongry.

"Ol' Brer Rabbit wuz so mad kaze he can't git no vittles nowhar and nohow, dat he kicked a cheer 'cross de room wid his hin' foot and skeered de young uns so dat dey flipped under de bed, an' dar dey stayed twel der daddy wuz out er sight an' hearin'.

"Brer Rabbit knowed mighty well dat 'twa'n't gwine ter do fer him ter be settin' roun' de house wid de fambly dat hongry dat dey can't skacely stan' 'lone. So he comb his hair, an' brush his hat, an' put on his mits fer ter keep de sun fum frecklin' his han's, an' tuck down his walkin' cane, an' put out down de road fer ter see what he kin see, an' hear what he kin hear."

At this point the children laughed, Sweetest Susan convulsively, and Buster John more sedately, yet heartily. Aunt Minervy Ann paused and regarded them with grave, inquiring eyes.

"What de matter now?" she asked solemnly. At this the children laughed louder than ever. "Well!" she cried, "ef you gwine ter have conniption fits, I 'll wait twel dey pass off."

"Why, I was laughing because you said Brother Rabbit put on his mits to keep his hands from freckling," explained Buster John; and Sweetest Susan, when she could catch her breath, declared that she was laughing for the same reason.

"You-all must be mighty ticklish," remarked

Aunt Minervy Ann, plucking at the dead grass. "I ain't see nothin' funny in dat. You nee' n't think dat rabbits is like dey uster be. Dey done had der day. In dem times dey growed big and had lots er sense, an' dey wuz mighty keerful wid deyself. But dey done had der day. Folks come 'long and tuck der place, an' since den dey done dwindle 'way twel dey ain't nothin' mo' dan runts, an' skacely dat. Folks holdin' de groun' now, but how long dey gwine ter hol' it? How long fo' sump'n else 'll come 'long an' take folks' place? De time may be short, er it may be long, but it 'll come — you min' what I tell you; an' when it do come, folks 'll dwindle 'way and git ter be runts des like de creeturs did, and dey 'll fergit how to talk so eve'ybody kin know what dey sayin'.

"Look at de creeturs! Why, de time wuz when dey could talk same ez folks, but now dey can't hardly jabber, and dey ain't nobody know what dey sayin' 'cept 't is dish yer A'on you got here" — the children looked at each other and smiled — "an' dat don't do him ner dem no good. Now des ez de creeturs is, de folks 'll be when de time come — you mark my word!"

"But all this time," remarked Buster John slyly, "the rabbits in the tale are suffering mightily for something to eat."

"Dat 's so, honey! I got so much on my min' dat I done clean fergit 'bout de tale. I wuz thinkin' 'bout de time when we-all, white and black, would be brung low. You 'll have to scuzen me, sho. Well, den, Ol' Brer Rabbit put on his mits and tuck down his walkin' cane, and went promenadin' down de big road. Ef he met anybody, dey never could gess dat he wuz mighty nigh famished, kaze he walk des es biggity es ef he des had de finest kinder dinner. He went on, smoothin' down his mustashes, when who should he meet but Brer Fox, wid a big basket on his arm.

"'Whar you been, Brer Fox?'

"'Loungin' roun'. Whar you gwine, Brer Rabbit?'

"'Up hill and down dale. What you got in yo' basket, Brer Fox?'

"'Des er hatful er goobers, Brer Rabbit.'

"'Parched, Brer Fox?'

"'Yes, indeedy, Brer Rabbit; parched good en brown.'

"'No, I thank you, Brer Fox; none fer me. Ef dey wuz fresh an' raw now, maybe I'd take some. But parched — my stomach won't stan' um. Mo' dan dat, I des had a bait er groun'-squir'l.'

"Now, Brer Rabbit wuz hankerin' atter de goobers so bad dat he can't stan' still, an' when he say groun'-squir'l, Brer Fox under-jaw drap an' 'gun ter trimble an' quiver. He say: —

"'Wuz he fat, Brer Rabbit?'

"'Fat ez a butter-ball, Brer Fox, but not too fat; dey wuz plenty er lean meat.'

"'My gracious, Brer Rabbit! Whar 'd you git 'im?'

"'Back up de road a piece, Brer Fox. A whole fambly un um stays dar.'

"'Show me de place, Brer Rabbit; my ol' 'oman been hankerin' atter groun'-squir'l fer de longest.'

"'I'll show you, Brer Fox; but yo' claws longer 'n mine, an' you 'll hatter do de grabblin'.'

"Brer Fox jaw shuck like he had a swamp chill. He 'low: 'You never is see nobody grabble, Brer Rabbit, twel you see me.'

"'I 'll stan' by, Brer Fox, an' see it well done.'

"Now, Brer Rabbit did know whar dey wuz a burrow er some kin', but he ain't know whedder it wuz a groun'-squir'l, er a wood-rat, er a highlan' moccasin. So he tuck Brer Fox up de big road a piece, and den dey struck out thoo de woods. But 'fo' dey start in de timber, Brer Rabbit 'low: —

"'You better hide yo' basket er goobers, Brer Fox, kaze it 'll bother you ter tote it thoo de bushes. I 'll watch you grabble, and I 'll keep my eye on de basket.'

"So said, so done. Brer Fox sot de basket down in de bushes, an' dey kivered it wid leaves and trash, and went on. Bimeby, dey got ter de place whar Brer Rabbit say de fambly er de groun'-squir'l live, an' he show Brer Fox de mouf er de burrow. Brer Fox 'low: —

"'It 'll be hard diggin', Brer Rabbit.'

"'De harder de diggin', Brer Fox, de bigger de crap. Dat 's what I hear um say.'

"Wid dat, Brer Fox shucked his coat, an' roll up his shirt-sleeves, an' start ter diggin'. He made de dirt fly. Atter while he stop ter rest and 'low: —

"'Keep yo' eye on my goobers, Brer Rabbit; don't let nobody run off wid um;' and den he sot in ter grabblin agin.

"'I'll watch um, Brer Fox; don't make no doubt er dat.'

"Den Brer Rabbit run to whar de basket wuz, flung de trash off 'n it, tuck it off in de woods a little piece, an' emptied all de goobers out 'n it. Den he fill it up wid sticks and chips, mos' ter de top, and on de trash he put a layer er goobers. Den he tuck it back and kivered it like twuz at fust, and went ter whar Brer Fox was grabblin'. Brer Fox 'low: —

"'You smell mighty strong er parched goobers, Brer Rabbit.'

"'I don't doubt dat, Brer Fox; I lifted de lid er de basket, fer ter see ef dey wuz all dar, an' de stench fum um come mighty nigh knockin' me down. Fer a minnit or mo' I wuz dat weak and sick I come mighty nigh gwine home.'

"Well, Brer Fox he grabble and grabble, twel he git tired er grabblin', and den he 'low dat he b'lieve he'll put off eatin' any groun'-squir'l twel some yuther day. Brer Rabbit say he kin do ez he please 'bout dat; an' den dey went on back ter whar dey lef' de basket. Brer Rabbit helt his nose an' lifted de lid an' looked in, an' 'low: —

"'Dey all dar, Brer Fox; you kin look for yo'self.'

"'I don't 'spute it, Brer Rabbit; I ain't say dey ain't all dar.'

"'Dat may be, Brer Fox, but I hear folks say you mighty 'spicious, an' I don't want nobody fer ter be 'spicionin' er me.'

"Brer Fox 'low: 'Don't kick fo' you er spurred, Brer Rabbit.'

"Brer Rabbit say, 'De right kinder horse don't need no spurrin', Brer Fox.'

"Well, Brer Fox picked up his basket an' went on home, an' Brer Rabbit he went de yuther way; but by de time Brer Fox git out er sight good, ol' Brer Rabbit run home, an' git a basket, an' run back ter whar he done hid de goobers, and 'twa'n't no time fo' he had um all at home, an' him an' his ol' 'oman an' de chillun had a reg'lar feastin' time.

"When Brer Fox foun' dat he had mo' trash dan goobers in his basket, he was dat mad dat he could 'a' bit hisse'f; but he ain't let on. He know dey ain't no use makin' no fuss, an' he know mighty well dat he can't ketch Brer Rabbit; he done tried dat befo'.

"So dis time he went ter law 'bout it. He laid de case 'fo' 'ol Judge Wolf, an' dey got out papers, an' sont atter Brer Rabbit. Well, dey want no gittin' 'roun' dat. Brer Rabbit had ter go; he wuz mighty skittish, but he knowed dat ef dey got de law on 'im he won't have no peace in dat settlement. So he went ter court, and dar he foun' a whole passel er de creeturs. When he got in, ol' Judge Wolf tuck his seat on de high flatform, an' put on his specs, an' started ter readin' in a great big book. Dey called de case, and Brer Fox tuck de stan' an' tol' his side; and den Brer Rabbit got up an' tol' his side. Judge Wolf tuck off his specs an' look at Brer Rabbit wid a broad grin. Den he ax Brer Fox how many goobers he had, and Brer Fox say he dunno how many, but dey must 'a' been a bushel. Judge Wolf ax 'im whar'bouts he got um. He say he got um frum a man on de river.

"Judge Wolf 'low, 'A man on de river! Well, ef dat de case you must 'a' had some sho 'nuff.' Den he turn ter Brer Rabbit an' 'low: 'Brer Rabbit, you'll hatter pay 'im his goobers back when you dig yo' crap.' Brer Rabbit say he 'll do de best he kin.

"Judge Wolf say, 'How 'll you have um, Brer Fox; raw er parched?'

"Brer Fox holler out, 'Parched, parched!'

"Judge Wolf 'low, 'Brer Rabbit, when you dig yo' crap, save all de parched goobers fer Brer Fox.'

"Brer Rabbit say he 'll be mo' dan glad ter do so, an' den dey 'journed de court-house."

"That 's what I call stealing," said Sweetest Susan emphatically, as Aunt Minervy Ann paused.

There was silence for awhile, and then Aunt Minervy Ann shook her head and said: "Ef folks had 'a' done dat away 't would 'a' been stealin', but de creeturs — dey got ways er dey own, honey. Dey dunno right fum wrong, an' ef dey did, 't would be mighty bad for we-all. Our own hosses 'ud kick us, and our own cows 'ud hook us, forty times a day. Dey would n't be no gittin' 'long wid um de way dey er treated."

"That 's so," said Buster John.

Just then Major Perdue came out on the back porch of the big house and called Aunt Minervy

Ann. It turned out that the two extra mules in the lot did belong to the major. He borrowed some harness and a wagon, and drove home with plenty of provisions, and with a comfortable sum of money which the children's grandfather had loaned him. Aunt Minervy Ann carried her cart back empty, but she did n't mind that. The children rode with her a little piece, and as a result had a very peculiar experience.

other. Aunt Minervy Ann was sure she heard it, and she declared that there was something wrong about the man; she could tell by his peculiar appearance.

So she advised the children to jump down and follow the wagon as far as their gate if no farther. They might find out something and be able to do somebody a good turn. Sweetest Susan did n't see the necessity of this, but Buster John was keen for anything that seemed to promise an adventure. He jumped from the cart and ran back after the wagon, while Sweetest Susan followed more leisurely. She followed fast enough, however, to catch up with the covered wagon, which was not going very rapidly. The wagon was the kind used by the North Carolina tobacco pedlers. The cover was higher at the ends than in the middle. The pole stuck out behind, and a water bucket was fastened to it. A trough for feeding the mules was swinging across the rear, and this with the jutting pole enabled Buster John to climb up and peer into the wagon. At first he saw nothing but a lot of bedclothes piled up on some bundles of fodder; but presently he heard sobbing again, and, looking closer, he saw a little child lying on its face in an attitude of despair.

At first Buster John thought of crawling into the wagon and asking the child what ailed it, but the man who was driving was in plain view, and, though Buster John was bold enough for a small boy, he was cautious too. The child seemed to be not more than two or three years old, and as it had on a frock Buster John could n't tell whether it was a boy or a girl. While he was considering what to do, the child raised its head, saw him, and wailed: "Oh, p'ease tate me out er here!" Buster John fell rather than jumped down, for he was afraid the man would see him. Presently the face of the child appeared at the back part of the wagon. At first it seemed that the little creature was preparing to jump out, but either fear overcame it, or the driver reached back and cut it with his whip, for it fell back with a loud wail of agony, a wail that sounded like the cry of some wild animal.

Sweetest Susan was ready to cry, her sympathies were so keen, but Buster John was angry. He ran to the front of the wagon and yelled at the man: —

"What 's the matter with your baby?"

"Hey?" responded the man. "Want a ride?

Of course you can ride; climb up. I ain't got time to stop."

"I said what's the matter with the baby, the baby in the wagon?" cried Buster John at the top of his voice.

"In the waggin? Oh, yes! Well, get in."

"Don't you do it, brother," said Sweetest Susan. "He heard what you said."

The man looked at them with twinkling eyes. "Oh, both want to ride. Well, get in — that's all I've got to say."

Buster John was not to be put down that way; he was very close to home now; in fact, he could see the tall form of his grandfather standing on the knoll above the spring, watching the covered wagon with curious eyes, for it had been a long day since one had come along that road going in that direction. So Buster John grew very bold indeed. He went close to the front wheel of the wagon, close to the heels of the off-mule.

"You know what I said. I asked you what was the matter with the baby in the wagon."

The man seemed to rouse himself. "Baby in the waggin! Why, they ain't no baby in there; it's a cat I picked up on the way. She's a mouser. We need mousers where I'm agoin'."

Buster John, more indignant than ever, ran ahead, called his grandfather, and asked him to go and see about the baby in the wagon, telling him hurriedly how queerly the man had acted.

But the White-Haired Master shook his head. "He 's only playing with you," he said.

The children were in despair at this, for they were sure that something was wrong. Even Aunt Minervy Ann had said so. Buster John began to pout, and Sweetest Susan was ready to cry. She looked appealingly at her grandfather, her eyes swimming in tears.

"What is it, Sweetest?" the White-Haired Master inquired.

"That poor little baby," she said, controlling herself the best she could; "I 'll dream about it all night."

"Well, don 't cry; we 'll see about it," remarked the grandfather soothingly.

By this time the wagon had come up. The driver bowed politely and would have gone on, but the White-Haired Master motioned him to stop. This he did, but with no good grace. He pulled up his mules, and sat on the seat expectantly, with a grin in his face that was half a scowl.

"You come from Milledgeville way?" the children's grandfather inquired.

"Who told you?" the man asked quickly; "them children there?"

"No," said the White-Haired Master, frowning a little. "I was simply inquiring."

The man laughed. "Well, I come from that-a-way."

"What news?" asked the White-Haired Master.

"Lots an' lots; I could n't tell you in a week. The wide world is turned end up'ards. Murderin', riot, bloodshed, burnin', rippin', rarin', roarin', snortin'. You know what?" The man closed his restless, roving eyes. "Well, down yon way they 're t'arin' up the railroad tracks while the brass ban' plays. I ketched 'em a doin' of it, an' I danced wi' 'em 'roun' the fire a time or two, an' then I picked up this waggin and mules and come on 'bout my business."

The man wagged his head up and down, and rolled it from side to side, and shifted his glances, and giggled in a very excited manner. The children's grandfather tried to find some basis for the man's strange actions; tried to duplicate them in his memory, but failed. Then he asked: —

"What have you in your wagon?"

"Well, fust an' last, I've got some few bed-cloze, an' some few ruffage for the mules; an' then — well, yes, there's a cat I picked up, a reg'ler mouser. She growls, but there ain't nothin' the matter wi' 'er."

In response to this statement the wagon cover was lifted high enough for the child to put its head out. Its little face was distorted with fear or despair.

"Me ain't no tat!" it cried; "my mammy say I'm her 'itty bitsy baby; my daddy say I'm his big 'itty man; my nunkey tall me Billy Bistit. Oh, p'ease lift me outer here. Me wanter see my daddy an' mammy!" The child had cried and screamed so much that its voice had a harsh and unnatural sound. It pierced the tender heart of the White-Haired Master like a knife and roused him to a fury of indignation.

"Is that what you call a cat, you trifling scoundrel?" he cried. He passed through the gate and was now close to the man.

"That's what," answered the man with a chuckle. "He'll bite, an' he'll scratch, an' he'll growl. An' he calls himself Billy Biscuit, but do he look like a biscuit? You would n't want me to call him a chicken, would you?"

He stuck out his tongue as he said this, and looked about as foolish as it is possible for a grown man to appear, and the grandfather's indignation changed to a feeling of amazement and disgust.

"Is the child yours?" he asked.

"Why, whose should he be, Mister? You 'd be errytated ef you wuz a youngster an' had to ride all day in a kivered waggin; now would n't you?"

The observation was a just one, considering the source; and though it lacked feeling and sympathy, the White-Haired Master could make no reply.

"This is a likely place to camp — in there by the spring," the man remarked. "Ef I thought I mought be so bold as to ax you" —

"You may," said the White-Haired Master. "Drive in the gate here and unhitch under the trees yonder. There 's fire under the wash-pot. You 'll find plenty of wood to start it up, but be careful about it; don 't burn any of the fencing."

The man drove in as directed, turned his wagon round, the tongue pointing to the gate, unhitched his mules, watered them without taking the harness off, and then gave them two bundles of fodder apiece to munch on. Then he got out his frying-pan, his skillet, and his coffee-pot, and finally proceeded to kindle a fire.

Buster John and Sweetest Susan watched all these proceedings with great interest, especially as the man paused every now and then to talk to himself. "Yes, that's me," he declared over and over again; "Roby Ransom, corridor 1, room 9."

He paid no attention to Buster John and Sweetest Susan, nor to Drusilla, who joined them as the wagon drove in the gate, and he seemed to have forgotten the child in the wagon. But Sweetest Susan had not forgotten it. She stood by the wagon and saw the little one looking at the man with frightened eyes.

The whole affair was very interesting to the children. The big trees had been a favorite resort for campers in old times, and the youngsters vaguely remembered seeing strange men sitting around the fire frying bacon that sent forth a very savory odor, but of late years there had been no campers there. The campers and wagoners, like most of the able-bodied men, had been camping out under the tents of the army or sleeping, as

Johnny Bapter put it, "under the naked canopies." Therefore this mysterious man was the first camper who had kindled a fire in the spring lot since Buster John, Sweetest Susan, and Drusilla had been of an age to appreciate the circumstance.

Consequently they watched him closely and in comparative silence, their comments being confined to low whispers. Sweetest Susan's solicitude was for the child in the wagon, but her curiosity compelled her to keep sharp eyes on the man, who went nervously about his business, and very awkwardly, too, as even the children could see. Sweetest Susan's solicitude was rewarded, for, as she leaned against the frame of the wagon, the child on the inside reached its soft little hands out and patted her gently on the arm. To Sweetest Susan this was more than a caress, and she seized the small hand and held it against her cheek for a moment. Then she made bold to ask the man — she called him Mr. Ransom at a venture — if she might bring the little one some supper.

"Who told you my name?" the man asked with suspicion in his eyes.

"I heard you call yourself Roby Ransom," replied Sweetest Susan very politely.

"Well, you heard right for once," he said. "Supper for the young-un? Tooby shore; fetch it. I did n't allow I'd take in boarders when I started, an' I ain't got any too much vittles for myself."

So Sweetest Susan and Drusilla went to the house to arrange for bringing the child some supper, while Buster John lagged behind and watched the man till the bell rang. Meanwhile the grandfather had told his daughter (the mother of Buster John and Sweetest Susan) about the child in the wagon, and that lady was in quite a fume about it. At first she insisted on going down and taking the child away from the man; she was sure there was something wrong.

"There may be," said the White-Haired Master, "but we are not sure about it, and we might make bad matters worse. There 's plainly something wrong about the man; that much is certain; but the child may be his, and it may be badly spoiled. No, it would be wrong to interfere with him; I 've thought it all over."

"If you'll take my advice," remarked his

daughter, "you 'll make the negroes tie the man and lock him in the corn-crib until we find out something about him."

"That would hardly be legal," said the old gentleman.

"Well, I don't think there is much law in the country at this time," the lady insisted. "If we knew he had stolen the child, what could you do with him?"

"What you say is very true," remarked the White-Haired Master; "truer even than you think it is. Still, there is no reason why we should be hasty and unjust."

As the lady was convinced against her will, she remained of the same opinion still, and that opinion became a conviction when Sweetest Susan arrived and told all she saw and all she thought. But there was nothing to be done but to give the child one full meal if it got no more, and so the lady set about fixing supper for the unfortunate. She piled a plate high with biscuits and ham and chicken, and when the children were through supper they waited patiently for Drusilla to finish hers, so they could all go together. Sweetest Susan insisted on carrying the plate herself.

When they arrived at the camper's fire, they found the man eating supper by himself.

"Where's the baby?" asked Sweetest Susan.

"In the waggin," replied the man curtly. "I wanted to take the imp out, but he would n't let me tetch him. Git him out, if you can."

The child needed no coaxing when Sweetest Susan called him. He crawled to the front of the wagon and held out his arms to her, and he hugged her so tightly around the neck that it was as much as she could do to climb down without falling. The little fellow was well dressed, but he was barefooted, and his feet were very cold.

"Where are his shoes?" asked Sweetest Susan indignantly.

"He must er pulled 'em off and flung 'em away. Oh, he's a livin' terror, he is. Don't you let him fool you."

The child ate his supper sitting in Sweetest Susan's lap, and he seemed to be very hungry. He tried to make Sweetest Susan eat some, too, and once or twice he smiled when she pretended to be eating ravenously. But for the most part the child kept his eyes fixed on Mr. Ransom, and clung more tightly to Sweetest Susan whenever he caught the man looking at him.

The result of it all was, that when the time came for the children to go to the house, Sweetest Susan found it impossible to get rid of the child. He would n't allow Ransom to take him — he seemed ready to go into convulsions whenever the man approached; and, finally, in order to induce him to get into the wagon, Sweetest Susan had to go in with him (accompanied by Drusilla) and once there, she was compelled to lie by the child until it dropped off to sleep. He held her hand tightly clasped in his tiny fists.

Buster John was impatient, and said he was going to bed, and Sweetest Susan told him to tell mamma that she and Drusilla would come as soon as the baby went to sleep. Drusilla, drowsy-eyed, lay down on the bedclothes and was asleep before the child was. Sweetest Susan made every effort to withdraw her hand and slip from the wagon, but these movements aroused the child, and set it to whimpering.

Everything was very still; even the frogs called to one another drowsily. The mules had cleaned up their ration of fodder, and were now dozing.

Under these circumstances, it was not long before Sweetest Susan was as sound asleep as Drusilla, and, apparently, the child was asleep, too.

Ransom in due time arose from the fire where he had been sitting, went to the rear of the wagon, looked in, and then stood listening intently. Nothing was to be heard but the regular, heavy breathing of three sound sleepers. He went to the spring, got some water, and carefully put out the fire. At no time had it been a large one. Then stealthily, almost noiselessly, he hitched the mules to the wagon, drove out at the gate and into the public road. Once Sweetest Susan dreamed that she was going to town in the wagon with Johnny Bapter; but that must have been when the wagon was going down the long and steep hill that led to Crooked Creek.

An hour after the wagon had disappeared, Mrs. Wyche, the children's mother, aroused herself from thoughts of her husband, who was in the army, and remembered that it was long past the time for Sweetest Susan to be in bed. She called to Jemimy, Drusilla's mother, who was nodding by the fire in the dining-room.

"Jemimy, go to the spring where the wagoner

is camping, and tell Sweetest Susan and Drusilla to come straight to the house; they should have been here long ago. Bring them with you."

Jemimy went to the spring, but saw no wagon nor any signs of one, the fire being out. She heard Johnny Bapter singing near the lot; she called him and asked about the wagon.

"Ef 'tain't down dar by de spring, I dunner whar 't is."

Jemimy ran back to the house, nearly frightened to death. Her report was: "Mist'iss, dey ain't no wagon dar!"

"Merciful heavens!" screamed the lady, "I told father to have the man tied and locked in the corn-crib, and now he has stolen my child! Oh, what shall I do?"

"An' he got Drusilla!" cried Jemimy, throwing up her hands wildly.

The White-Haired Master came forth from the library with a troubled face. He was a man of action, and in five minutes the whole plantation was aroused. But Sweetest Susan and Drusilla had disappeared. Strong-lunged negroes called them, but they made no answer. They were several miles away and fast asleep.

"DEY AIN'T NO WAGON DAR!"

IV.

SWEETEST SUSAN'S STRANGE ADVENTURE.

THE White-Haired Master was a man of action, but one was before him. As soon as Johnny Bapter heard Jemimy's inquiry, and found that the wagon had disappeared, he ran to Aaron's cabin with the news. Instantly the Son of Ben Ali was on his feet and running. Straight to the horse-lot he went, where he gave a peculiar call, and one of the horses came galloping to him, whinnying. There was a clinking of harness, a rush to the carriage house, and in two minutes the rattle of buggy wheels was heard on the gravel. By the time the White-Haired Master could get his overcoat on and fix himself for facing the cold, crisp air, the buggy was at the back gate with Aaron calling, "All ready, Master."

He had no need to repeat the call. The children's grandfather came running down the steps very nimbly for one of his years, and in a moment was in the buggy, with Aaron beside him.

"Are you going?" he asked.

"Yes, Master," replied the son of Ben Ali.

"I 'm mighty glad of it," remarked the White-Haired Master. "Where are the reins?"

"In the saddle ring; I forgot to take 'em out." He spoke to the horse, and the animal broke from a walk into a canter, shaking its head playfully. By this time, Johnny Bapter, armed with a flaming torch, was more than halfway to the side gate, where the wagon had come in and gone out. He reached the gate as the buggy drove up, and Aaron seized the torch and examined the ground. He saw the wagon tracks coming in, and saw where it turned as it went out. He spoke to the horse as he flung the torch away, and climbed into the buggy as it moved off. He spoke once more, and the animal broke into what seemed to be a wild gallop, going so rapidly that the buggy appeared to be in the air when it went whirling over a sunken place in the road. On level stretches the horse ran as a racer runs, and the wheels of the buggy gave forth an undertone that sounded like the droning of a swarm of bees.

"How do you drive without the lines?" the White-Haired Master asked, when he became convinced that the son of Ben Ali had the horse under complete control.

"He knows me, Master, and I know him," replied Aaron.

It was not a satisfactory answer, perhaps, but it seemed to be sufficient. Up hill the horse, which was a strong one, went with a long, swinging trot. The top reached, the trot would be exchanged for a gallop. This went on for some time, until Aaron vetoed the gallop. When they had gone on for an hour, and were nearly to Harmony Grove, a small settlement about ten miles from the Abercrombie place, the Son of Ben Ali stopped the horse, jumped from the buggy, and carefully examined the road ahead, getting down on his hands and knees to do so.

He rose and shook his head, and walked slowly back to the buggy.

"What is the matter?" the White-Haired Master asked.

"The wagon ain't come 'long here, Master. The wheel tire is two inches wide. No track like that in the road."

"It was an army wagon," said the grandfather musingly. "What has become of it? It must have passed here. The first fork in the road is at Harmony Grove. We'll go there."

So they drove on to Harmony Grove. As it happened there was a sort of social gathering in the schoolhouse. As always happens on such occasions, there were several young men and boys who were too shy to venture in the house where the girls and young women were. If a wagon or vehicle of any kind had passed, they surely would have seen it. But no wagon had passed.

Such of them as had horses volunteered to join the searching party, but the White-Haired Master thanked them. If the wagon had n't passed, it was still on the road somewhere, and he and Aaron would find it. Indeed, the White-Haired Master had made a calculation. Harmony Grove was ten miles from his place. He had come the distance in something less than an hour, and it was now ten o'clock. If the wagon had left the spring at eight o'clock it could hardly have reached Harmony Grove before then. Aaron judged that they should have overtaken the wagon about six miles from the spring.

As a matter of fact, they had overtaken the wagon and passed it, five and one half miles from home, or, to be more exact, at the humble residence of Mr. Barlow Bobs. They had passed the wagon without knowing it, for the reason that the vehicle was not in sight from the road, and they would have passed it in broad daylight.

The driver, Mr. Roby Ransom — that was really his name, as it turned out — had not gone more than two miles from the Abercrombie place before the desire to sleep overcame him, and he began to nod. For a while he would nod, and then rouse himself; but finally he leaned against the framework, over which the cover was spread, and began to sleep soundly. The lines slipped from his hands, but caught on the brake and hung there, too high for the feet of the mules to become entangled in them.

When the wagon came to the top of the long hill that slopes down to Crooked Creek, the mules were surprised to feel no restraining hands on the reins. At first they hardly knew what to do, but they were well trained, and they held back the wagon until near the bottom, and then they broke into a swift trot and went swishing through the shallow waters of Crooked Creek. Without a pause they pulled the wagon sedately up the opposite hill, which was not a very steep one. They remained in the road as became sensible mules, but they grew more and more uncertain in their movements as they realized that no hand was guiding them.

Finally they came to the humble home of Mr. Bobs — or, rather, they came to the short lane that led to Mr. Bobs's log cabin. Into this they turned, the hub of the hind wheel missing the fence corner by the breadth of a hair. Pursuing this road, they followed it into Mr. Bobs's back yard; and they finally drew up behind the corn-crib, a double-pen built of logs. As there was a fat fodder stack behind this crib, the mules concluded that they would put up for the night. After this, the only movement they made was to see-saw the wagon as they reached for the fodder, and to snort occasionally when too much dust from the forage crept up their nostrils.

Once, about five minutes after the mules had reached this harbor, they pricked up their ears at the sound of a running horse whirling a buggy along the road, and Mr. Bobs's house-dog barked dubiously, but beyond this there was nothing to bother them, and no alarming noises were heard. Sweetest Susan, Little Biscuit, and Drusilla were sound asleep, and so was Mr. Roby Ransom. It was a good thing for Mr. Ransom that he was asleep, for there is no doubt that if the White-Haired Master had come up with him on the road he would have fared but ill. But Providence seemed to have taken him under its wing.

The White-Haired Master concluded to wait in the neighborhood of Harmony Grove until dawn, knowing that nothing could be done in the darkness. It was a long, long night. The grandfather walked up and down, up and down, the whole time, and though the Son of Ben Ali sat in the schoolhouse as still as a statue, he was as impatient as the Master. He had built a fire in the old sheet-iron stove, and the draft rushing into this puffed like a locomotive, and, for a while, kept time with the tramp, tramp, tramp, of the grandfather.

But dawn came at last, and as soon as things were visible, the two were in the buggy and away. When they had gone two or three miles toward home, Aaron jumped from the buggy and strolled on ahead of the horse. It was quite light by this time, and he scanned the road carefully, searching for the tracks made by the big wheels of the army wagon. He could not find them where they were not, but when he came to the short lane that led to Mr. Bobs's house, he saw where the wagon had turned in. Making sure that it had not come out again, he waited for the White-Haired Master to come up. He said not a word, but pointed to the tracks made by the wheels.

Now, it happened that Mr. Bobs had his sister, Miss Elviry, for his housekeeper. Miss Elviry was forty-odd years old, and quite independent of servants, and it was her habit to rise at daybreak, summer and winter, kindle into a blaze the fire that had been wrapped in a blanket of ashes the night before, and proceed to cook an early breakfast, so that her brother might get to work at his turning-lathe, or his broom-making, as soon as possible. Miss Elviry went to bed early and rose early, as a matter of both conscience and habit. But on this particular morning she rose earlier than usual. She had a "feelin'," as she afterward expressed it, that everything was not all right. Once or twice, when she woke during the night, she heard the house dog uttering smothered growls and whining, a certain sign that everything was not as it should be. She refrained from rousing her brother, but she had a good mind to. She made up for her restraint in this matter, however, by rising half an hour earlier herself. She kindled a fire, put on a supply of wood to keep it going, and hurriedly dressed herself. Then, although the stars were shining, she unbolted the back door and looked out. The little outhouse in which Mr. Bobs did his work and kept his tools barred her vision, but she heard unusual noises, such as the rattling of chains and the creaking of harness and the snorting of horses or mules.

Now, Miss Elviry was not a timid woman. She had some of the independence and energy that would have made her brother more prosperous had he possessed a fair share of them. So, while she was astonished at the noises she heard, she was not alarmed. Instead of rushing into her brother's room to arouse him, she seized the axe, which was always brought in over night in case of an emergency, and sallied out to see what it was that had taken possession.

The house dog heard her, and came out from under the house fairly screaming with delight, for he had had a horrible night of it. Feeling himself adequately reinforced by Miss Elviry's presence, his bristles rose, and he rushed around the outhouse and proceeded to bay the back end of the wagon with the greatest fury, and his indignation grew even greater when he heard Miss Elviry's firm voice urging him to "Sic 'em, Spot! Sic 'em!"

The voice aroused Sweetest Susan, but did not seem to disturb the other sleepers. The child rubbed her eyes, but for a long moment she could not imagine where she was. Then she remembered she was in the wagon when she should be at home in bed. And, "Oh, what will mamma say?" Dawn, still glimmering far away, sent a gleam of light into the wagon, and toward this Sweetest Susan groped her way, stumbling over Drusilla, who merely turned over with a sigh that sounded like a groan.

"Who are you, anyhow?" cried Miss Elviry sharply.

"Oh, it's only me!" answered Sweetest Susan, whose head and shoulders were dimly outlined

"OH, WHAT WILL MAMMA SAY?"

against the interior darkness of the wagon. "Take me out, please. Oh, this is not home! Where am I?"

Miss Elviry went nearer; there was something about the child's voice that drew her. "Oh, hush up, Spot!" she cried to the dog; "now you 've started, you 'll never stop." She went close to the wagon end and looked at the child as well as she could. "What 's your name, honey?"

Now, as soon as Miss Elviry came nearer, the child's sharper vision recognized her. She made quilts, and wove counterpanes for people who were comfortably well off, and she had in this way been a frequent visitor at the Abercrombie place.

"Is that you, Miss Elviry? Please take me out!"

Miss Elviry was thunderstruck, as she said afterwards.

"Well, ef that ain't—Why! Well I know the end of the world ain't fur off now! Susan Wyche, what are you doin' in this rig at this time of day, when by good rights you ought to be at home in bed?"

"Take me out, please, Miss Elviry; and don't

scold. I 'm going to run to the house as hard as I can."

"Ef you are talkin' about your own house, you 'll have to do some extry hard runnin' ef you get there by dinner time. You 'll go into this house right here. 'T ain't so big an' fine, but the fire in there is just as warm, and your hands are like ice."

So she carried Sweetest Susan in the house, put a pillow in the chair, "to make it feel like home," as she said, and stationed the child in the warmest corner. Then she woke her brother. "Do your dressin' in your own room," she said; "we 've got comp'ny this mornin'."

Mr. Bobs did n't seem to relish this, and he began to grumble in tones too low to be heard in the adjoining room. "Comp'ny! Well, be jing'd ef they ain't afoot early! That 's all I 've got to say, bejing'd ef 't ain't." And that was all Mr. Bobs did say.

Sweetest Susan soon informed Miss Elviry of the facts as she knew them, and then remembered that Drusilla was still in the wagon — and the cute little baby — yes, and that awful man.

Mr. Bobs was very much surprised to see Sweetest Susan in that place at that early hour, and glad, too, for he and the Abercrombies and the Wyches had always been good friends.

"You know what it says in the Bible, Elviry; fust war, and then signs and wonders. That 's what it says, bejinged ef 'tain't." In a few moments Mr. Bobs was put in possession of such facts as his sister had learned, and the fifty-odd queer conclusions her quick imagination had conjured into being.

It was quite light now, and Mr. Bobs, selecting a stout hickory cane from his collection, sallied out, remarking: "He 's got to be a heap bigger than me ef I don't find out why he 's creepin' 'roun' a-stealin' children, and why he 's crope into my premises. Bejing'd ef he ain't."

But as Mr. Bobs went out, the White-Haired Master drove into the lane, and he and Aaron came forward as rapidly as they could. Mr. Bobs went to the wagon, turned the heads of the mules away from the fodder stack, and then looked into the wagon. Drusilla and Little Biscuit were soundly sleeping, but nothing was to be seen of the driver. Searching around the premises carefully and continuously, Mr. Bobs presently heard a voice in a pine thicket not far away, and there was Mr. Roby Ransom preaching a sermon to the birds and bushes. He was not preaching loudly, for he seemed to be exhausted, and occasionally he leaned against a sapling for support.

Mr. Bobs knew him at once as a crazy man who had lived in the neighborhood some years before, and who had been sent to the asylum from an adjoining county.

Meanwhile the White-Haired Master and the Son of Ben Ali came up, and great was their consternation for a moment when they discovered that neither Sweetest Susan nor the wagoner were to be seen. Fortunately, the suspense of the grandfather was of short duration. He heard Sweetest Susan call his name, and in a moment she was in his arms, and Miss Elviry found it necessary to wipe her specs.

Then came Mr. Bobs with an explanation of the whole matter; and he and the White-Haired Master and Aaron went to secure the unfortunate Mr. Ransom.

"Roby, you better come go with us, I reckin," said Mr. Bobs kindly, laying his hand on Ransom's shoulder; "come, now, you better go 'long wi' us."

But the unfortunate had worked himself into a state of frenzy. He glared at the three with glassy eyes, and then, shrieking out something about the fiend Apollyon, ran through the bushes and brambles into the woods. Not even Aaron could overtake him. He disappeared, and although searching parties scoured the woods for miles around, the unfortunate was never seen again. His fate became a legend, and the legend developed into the collection of myths which in that neighborhood are passed about from mouth to mouth to this day. Those most affected by the whites tell of Robber Ransom, while those of the negroes give blood-curdling tales about Robityransom. Some of these tales are curious, while all are marvelous, and parts of other myths and legends have been injected into them.

It is hardly necessary to say that neither the White-Haired Master nor Aaron made any serious effort to find the lunatic after he had once disappeared. They had other things to think about. There was Sweetest Susan's mother; they knew that every hour that passed without their return was to her a long season of agony. The Son of Ben Ali, indeed, made no delay about going.

There would not be room in the buggy for four, in any event, and by taking advantage of the neighborhood by-paths and short cuts, he could reduce the distance by at least a mile and a half.

The White-Haired Master delayed no longer than was necessary. Mr. Bobs and Miss Elviry insisted that he should have a bit to eat. "Ef 't ain't fine, it 's clean, thank goodness!" she exclaimed. But no; he smiled at Miss Elviry's remark and declared that he would have no appetite until he saw Sweetest Susan safe in her mother's arms. Drusilla heard the remark, and wondered if she'd be safe in her mammy's arms; and after thinking over it awhile she concluded that she 'd be far from safe at this time. Jemimy's affection was strong enough, but it had very sharp reactions when her alarm was over.

There were still two matters to settle. The first made its appearance in the back of the wagon, while the White-Haired Master was thanking Miss Elviry for her proffered breakfast. It was little Billy Biscuit, who thumped on the wagon gate and cried: —

"Please tate me down. Me want my bekkus. Me 'mell meat a-f'yin'."

"Did you ever, in all your born days!" exclaimed Miss Elviry. Then she ran to the wagon, smiled at the child, and little Billy Biscuit laughed back at her. When she took him in her arms, he put his small arms around her neck and hugged her so hard that he grunted. It was evidently a trick that his mother had taught him, and a very cute one it was. This time, when Miss Elviry laughed, she blushed.

"You need n't be amazed at the blushin'," remarked Mr. Bobs to the White-Haired Master; "she ain't been hugged afore, not sence — well, not sence I dunno when."

Miss Elviry's only reply to this was to kiss the baby and squeeze him the more closely to her breast. Now, when Sweetest Susan saw little Billy Biscuit, it caused her a sharp pang of remorse to feel that she had almost forgotten the poor little thing. She ran to him now, and would have taken him in her arms, but he, thinking she was up for a frolic, kicked his feet, laughing and screaming in glee, and clung to Miss Elviry.

Nevertheless, the child was a problem. What was to be done with him? It was plain that Ransom, the lunatic, perhaps feeling the need of company, had taken him on the road. To explain the child's presence, however, did n't settle the matter. He was there, and what was to be done with him? Miss Elviry solved the problem.

"May n't I keep him 'till his kinnery come?" she insisted.

"Less'n he begins for to blate an' squall at night," remarked Mr. Bobs laughing.

But Miss Elviry was very earnest about it, and so it was arranged.

"And we can come and see him sometimes," said Sweetest Susan, with an eye to the future.

"Yes; and when you come, fetch a lot of old clothes that used to belong to you an' your brother, ef your ma 's got any to spare," replied Miss Elviry, with an eye to the practical.

There was another problem — the wagon and mules. "Ef them mules has swallowed one bundle of fodder, they 've walloped up a hunderdweight," remarked Mr. Bobs, when the subject of the wagon was mentioned. It was finally decided that he was to take charge of the vehicle and team, and if no one called for them, they were to be his.

V.

A VISIT TO BILLY BISCUIT.

As the kidnapped children were preparing to get in the buggy, Drusilla made this remark to Sweetest Susan: —

"Ef mammy don't kill me dis day, it'll be kaze I'm dead when I git dar."

At home Jemimy was walking up and down wringing her hands, and making statements that went far to show that Drusilla knew pretty well what to expect.

"I ain't sleep a wink dis night, less'n you can call noddin' sleepin'; not a wink; an' when I does git holt er dat gal, I'm gwineter make her wish she'd 'a' stayed los'."

"Just because she stayed with Sweetest Susan, I suppose," said Mrs. Wyche.

"No'm, not 'zactly dat," replied Jemimy; "but why n't she come on ter de house an' fetch little Mistiss wid 'er? She plenty big 'nuff fer dat. Ef she 'd 'a' come, little Mistiss would 'a' come; you know dat you'se'f. Oh, ef I don't pay dat nigger gal back fer de ol' and de new!"

"You 'd better thank the Lord, if you ever see her again," said Sweetest Susan's distressed mother.

"I 'll do dat, ma'am; I 'll thank 'im on my bended knee; an' fo' I git it onbent good, I 'll lay dat gal 'crost it; an' when I git done wid 'er, she won't git in no mo' waggins — she won't git tuck off by nobody, not twel she 's done grown, er atter dey done put me on de coolin-board. I may not know how ter raise childun, but I know how to make um stan' 'roun'."

All this time Mrs. Wyche was lying upon a sofa in a state of collapse, while Jemimy, more vigorous (or more venomous, as she would have put it), was walking up and down in the long hallway, wringing her hands and groaning.

Morning came on, and it was light enough to put out the candles, but they were left burning. Presently a modest ray of sunlight crept in and played upon the wall opposite. It seemed to be a signal, for the moment Mrs. Wyche's eyes fell upon it, she heard a sharp knock at the door.

Jemimy heard it, too, and ran to push back the thumb-bolt. Quick as she had been, Mrs. Wyche was by her side as she opened the door. Aaron was standing on the threshold. Mrs. Wyche held her breath as he raised his hand, and Jemimy leaned against the wall with a moan.

"All safe, all safe, Mistiss. They 're comin' in the buggy." To Jemimy he said: "Get breakfast — get breakfast! they 're all hungry."

"Did you go with father?" Mrs. Wyche asked.

"Yes, Mistiss."

"I knew it," said the lady. The tone of her voice was full of the liveliest gratitude. Aaron bent his head, raised his hand, and was gone before they could ask any particulars.

Mrs. Wyche would have called him back, but at that moment she heard the sound of buggy wheels, and she knew that the kidnapped children had arrived. Before she could dry her eyes, Sweetest Susan came running in and rushed into her mother's arms with a glad cry; whereupon the mother felt called upon to weep a little more; though the tears that fell now were far different from those that fell in the dreary watches of the night.

Drusilla came in with less confidence. She was not sure of her reception. "Howdy, mammy? Howdy, Mistiss?" she said, and then looked at Jemimy.

"Come yer, gal!" said Jemimy. She turned Drusilla around and inspected her carefully. "You ain't hurt nowhar, is you?"

"No'm!" exclaimed Drusilla. Then another thought struck her. "Mammy, did you cry much kaze I was done losted?"

"What I had ter cry fer?" exclaimed Jemimy.

"Well, ef you 'd 'a' been losted, I 'd 'a' cried," remarked Drusilla.

At this Jemimy broke down. "Look yer, nigger! You better stop foolin' wid me. De nex' time you do like you done done, I 'm gwinter kill you. You hear dat?"

Whereupon Jemimy flouted out and went into the kitchen, where she went about breakfast with surprising energy, talking to herself all the time.

It is impossible to describe the keen disappointment of Buster John when he came down to breakfast and learned of the remarkable events of the night. He was disappointed, first, because he had not been kidnapped with the rest; and, second, because he had not been waked to join in the search. He had an idea that he had been treated unfairly, not by any particular person or persons, but in some way. It was just his luck, he said, to be left out when anything very interesting was going to happen. He recalled the day he remained at home from school on some slight excuse, and a pack of hounds ran a gray fox right up to the schoolhouse door and caught it there; and a little later the same day the boys found a partridge nest right on the verge of the playground, and the nest had seventeen beautiful eggs in it. There were other occasions that he remembered, and he said to himself and to others that it was pretty hard that a girl should be having such a fine time while he was asleep in bed.

But Sweetest Susan declared that it was n't such a fine time after all. She was asleep, and did n't know anything about it. Nevertheless, she felt that she had grown in importance by taking part in the adventure, and she put on some of those airs which are very cute in girls of her age, but which are — well, not so cute in grown women.

Buster John submitted to them with very good grace, considering that he was a spirited boy.

He knew he would have done some strutting himself if Sweetest Susan's adventures had been his. As it was, he contented himself with assertions as to what he would have done had he been in the wagon. He might have gone to sleep at first, he said, but just as sure as anything he would have waked when the wagon jolted over a rock or a lump in the road, and then — well, suffice it to say, that wagoner would have found himself in deep trouble. Buster John would have pulled out his pistol —

"Why, you have n't any pistol; you know you have n't," cried Sweetest Susan.

"Well, I 'd have had one if I had been in the wagon. I would have guessed what was going to happen."

"How come you did n't?" inquired Drusilla, at this point. "Why n't you guess we wuz gwine ter drop off to sleep? An' why n't you stay down dar an' wake we-all up? I don't like dish yer kinder guessin' what guesses when dey ain't no need er guessin'."

But Buster John insisted that he would have borrowed his grandfather's pistol, and hid himself in the wagon; and when they came to some dark and lonely spot in the road, then and there he would have demanded satisfaction.

"Huh! He 'd 'a' gi' you sati'faction!" exclaimed Drusilla. "He 'd 'a' grabbed you an' rolled yo' head in one er dem blankets, an' ef dat ain't sati'fy you, he 'd 'a' gi' you sump'n else."

"That 's all you know about pistols," said Buster John imperiously.

"No needs ter know 'bout pistols," replied Drusilla, "when you know 'bout folks. Why, honey, dat ar man would 'a' eat you up ef you dez so much ez bat yo' eye at 'im. Ain't I done see de way he chaw vittles, an' how he talk 'long wid hisse'f?"

Nevertheless, Buster John insisted that he would have rescued the captives and brought them home in triumph.

As may be supposed, the strange adventure of Sweetest Susan and Drusilla afforded a subject for a great deal of gossip on the plantation and in the surrounding country, and the children themselves passed many a pleasant hour in discussing it, when otherwise they would have been very lonely. Sweetest Susan often thought of little Billy Biscuit, and once, when talking about him to her mother, she mentioned what Miss Elviry had said about children's cast-off clothes. Now, as it happened, there was a chestful of clothes somewhere about the house, and Mrs. Wyche made haste to hunt it up and sort out as much as might be of some service to the little waif. Then, woman-like, having her mind on the matter, she insisted that the clothes must be sent as soon as possible, and gave orders that Johnny Bapter should carry everything the next morning.

The children, hearing of this, insisted that they be allowed to go along, and as there was nothing to prevent (Sherman's army having unwittingly dispersed school and schoolmaster) it was arranged that Johnny Bapter should use the spring wagon, which had two seats, so that Buster John, Sweetest Susan, and Drusilla could all go along. And as Johnny Bapter was going that far, he might as well take an early start and go on to Harmony Grove, to carry some gifts of butter, flour, and other supplies to an old friend of Mrs. Wyche, whose husband was in the army, and whose sources of maintenance had been all but swept away by the army of invasion.

The children were up bright and early, but

they found Johnny Bapter and the wagon waiting for them. There was not much delay after that, you may be sure; only a little wait on Drusilla, who was not likely to allow so short a journey to interfere with the play of her appetite. Buster John and Sweetest Susan went out to the wagon with half their breakfast in their hands. Johnny Bapter took off his hat to them very politely, and then, when they were seated in the wagon, he took off his hat and bowed twice.

"You 're mighty polite this morning, Johnny Bapter," said Buster John. "What 's the matter with you?"

"Well, fust I bow ter you-all, an' den I bow ter dem ar waffles an' dat ar ham. I ain't see no waffles in so long dat I bleege ter bow at um. Dey may not know me, but I knows dem."

That settled it, of course. Johnny Bapter knew what he was doing. In their exuberant spirits the children would have given him all their waffles and ham, but no: "I ain't no ways greedy," said Johnny Bapter, so he only took two thirds. "An' de waffles got butter on um!" he exclaimed. "I 'm mighty glad you-all tuck a notion to go 'long. Look like dey ain't been no war when you kin git a tas'e er waffles. Git up dar, hoss! what you holdin' back on level groun' fer, when you know I'm up here eatin' waffles? Ef anybody ax you-all how come I don't b'long ter no church, you up an' tell um dat it's des kaze I ain't hear none er de preachers say dey gwinter be waffles up dar whar good folks goes. Ef dey'll des say 'waffles,' I'm wid um, an' I'll stay wid um, too; don't you disremember dat —

'Fer John-nee Bapiter is my name —
You ax my mammy, she 'll tell you de same!'"

This last was a snatch of song that sounded sweetly on the morning air. It was accompanied by a shaking of the reins that set the horse trotting at the top of his speed. In a very short while, as it seemed to the children, who enjoyed the ride, they were at Mr. Bobs's, where they were met by Miss Elviry, who said she was delighted to see them. The clothes she declared the very thing, every stitch being in the right place, and each garment certain to fit to a t-wy-ty — some might be a little too big now, at the present time, but they would n't stay too big many days.

"Somethin' told me you-all was a-comin' to-day. I had a ringin' in my right ear, an' my nose has been a-eetchin' ever sence I got up this mornin'. I know'd I was certain to have company, and who could it be, says I to myself, but the youngsters from the Abercrombie place?"

"How is Little Billy Biscuit?" asked Sweetest Susan.

"As fine as split silk," responded Miss Elviry with a fond laugh; "as fat as a pig, and the cutest thing you ever laid eyes on. Come right in; he 's back in here some'rs. Billy! Billy Biscuit! Where are you, for goodness' sake?"

"Here me!" replied Billy.

"Come here," said Miss Elviry; "here 's somebody wants to see you."

"Uh-uh! Me tan't; me 's a moo-talf. Moo-talf in de pen — tan't dit out."

When Miss Elviry and the children went to see what Billy was up to, they found that he had turned a chair on its side, and with that had penned himself in a corner of the room.

"Moo-talf want water," he exclaimed. Miss Elviry would have given him some from the gourd, but he protested loudly. "N-o-o-o! Moo-talf d'ink out de pan," and nothing would do but he must have a pan of water. From this he drank as he had seen the calf drink.

"Did anybody ever see the like of that?" exclaimed Miss Elviry in an ecstacy of pride. "They ain't narry 'nother child in the world, his age and inches, half as smart as he is."

Billy Biscuit acted as if he thought so too. Inside the somewhat narrow limits of his pen, he walked to and fro on his all-fours, as if trying to show himself off.

Now, Miss Elviry could say nothing on behalf of Billy Biscuit's accomplishments that Sweetest Susan would not agree to. She was very fond of babies and young children, and had a peculiar knack of entertaining them. She felt, too, a special interest in Billy Biscuit, having been the means of rescuing him from that unfortunate lunatic, and so she sat on the floor by the little fellow, and in a very few minutes they were having great fun. Especially was it great fun when Drusilla joined them and solemnly pretended to have a fit. Billy Biscuit laughed until he was nearly exhausted at Drusilla's queer antics, so that, finally, Miss Elviry felt compelled to beg

A WILD BEAST OF THE FOREST, NAME UNKNOWN

her not to be so funny. Whereupon Drusilla became really solemn. Her clownish antics were put aside, and she became a wild beast of the forest, name unknown. She went about the room on hands and knees, growling and making strange noises in her throat. Those were thrilling moments for Billy Biscuit when this wild animal headed in his direction, and he would rush to the protection of Sweetest Susan with just that tinge and taste of fear that gave a peculiar zest to the play.

As for Buster John, he had other fish to fry, as Miss Elviry said. Lucky for him, Mr. Bobs had cut one of the fingers of his right hand the afternoon before, and the cut had developed such soreness that he was taking a day off. Buster John, in looking about the place, which was a small one indeed, but very interesting, had come upon Mr. Bobs sitting in the door of his little workshop smoking his clay pipe — one that he had made himself, for he was a very ingenious man.

"Howdy, Mr. Bobs?" said Buster John, with as much politeness as a small boy can muster.

"Why, howdy?" replied Mr. Bobbs. "You 're

young Abercrombie — no — Wyche. Well, 't ain't much of a mistake to put you wi' the 'Crombies. The Wyche in you don't hurt you. You 're a 'Crombie all over, ef I ever seed one, an' I 've seed 'em all, fust an' last."

As Mr. Bobs sat looking at Buster John, he presented a very picturesque figure. Though the weather was a trifle chilly, he sat without his coat, and the sleeves of his shirt were rolled up, exposing half of his brawny, sunburnt arms. His wool hat sat on the back of his head, showing a high forehead. He wore a full beard and no moustache, and his eyes twinkled with both humor and shrewdness.

"What 's this I hear about Mr. Thimblefinger and all them rigamaroles?" he asked, after a while.

Buster John swelled with conscious knowledge, but he did not commit himself. "I 'm sure I don't know," he replied. "What did you hear?"

"A mighty heap of things," said Mr. Bobs; "lots more than I can take time to relate."

"Who told you, Mr. Bobs?" Buster John was very cautious.

"Them that told me was n't tellin' tales out of

school. But fust and fo'most, how come you to know Mr. Thimblefinger?"

"We — we just found him," replied Buster John.

"Ketched him out!" said Mr. Bobs, laughing at the thought of such a thing. "I allowed maybe that was the way of it. Well, you an' your little Sis is mighty lucky chaps."

"Drusilla was with us," Buster John explained.

"The nigger gal? H'm — well, yes — I reckon so," remarked Mr. Bobs with a frown. "Well, maybe white folk 'll have a breathin' spell now that the whole kit and bilin' is free."

Mr. Bobs's prejudice made no impression on Buster John. "What has become of Little Mr. Thimblefinger?" he inquired. "I asked Aaron, but he only shook his head."

"He ain't no nigger, I 'll be boun'," suggested Mr. Bobs.

"Who? Aaron? He 's an Arab."

"I hear tell," remarked Mr. Bobbs, "that away back yander, the Arabs was a' right sight pearter than our folks. They know'd all about physic and algeber, an' things like that. Now, I reckin you think that Aaron is e'en about the smartest man in the world. Come, now! Don't you? Hey?"

Buster John reflected awhile, and then replied: "Not the smartest man in the world."

"Well, anyhow, you 've got the idee strong in your mind that he 's a heap the smartest man anywhere in these diggin's: now, hain't you?" persisted Mr. Bobs.

Buster John did not assent to this in so many words, but his tone and manner left no doubt on Mr. Bobs's mind that the youngster had very extreme opinions as to Aaron's gifts.

"I don't blame you," said Mr. Bobs. "You 're young yit, an' you hain't traveled much the wide world all over. To-day 's e'en about the fust time you 've been to our house sence you weighed a pound more than a 'possum. I want to show you a thing or two. You 've got the idee, an' your Sis, too, I reckon, that Aaron knows it all. Ef you 'll call her out, I 'll show you that Aaron don't know more than half of the things that mought be know'd."

Buster John called Sweetest Susan, and she came running out, followed by Drusilla.

"Stand a little furder back," said Mr. Bobs,

"HE'S GOING TO SHOW US SOMETHING"

motioning with his hands; "a little furder yit; now, that 'll do. Keep your eyes open."

There was no need for that suggestion. "He 's going to show us something," Buster John explained, and then the children stood still and watched, hardly drawing breath.

VI.

MR. BOBS AND HIS BUBBLE.

The children stood watching Mr. Bobs attentively, their attitude betraying their curiosity and doubt. They were anxious to see how Mr. Bobs could convince them that there were smarter men than Aaron in that neighborhood, and doubtful of his ability to do so. It was plain that Mr. Bobs himself did not share their doubts. He was in no hurry, and yet there was no delay in his movements; he was slow but methodical. He knocked the ashes from his pipe and carefully cleaned it out with his pocket knife, blowing through the stem to clear away all particles of tobacco. This done, he laid the pipe carefully on the step beside him, reached into the room behind him, and drew forth a wash-pan that seemed to be a little more than half full of soapy water. There was also in the pan a small wooden paddle. With this Mr. Bobs whipped the soapy water gently, and the children noticed that instead of breaking into a foamy mass of bubbles, as soapy water does, three or four large bubbles appeared.

This result seemed to be unsatisfactory to Mr. Bobs. He drew forth from an inside pocket of his coat a large leather or morocco pocketbook, and began to search through its various compartments. He finally found what he was searching for — a little paper packet, wrapped round and round with many yards of white sewing thread. This thread Mr. Bobs unwound very carefully. Then, unfolding the paper, he took therefrom the merest pinch of white powder, and flirted it into the pan of water from his fingers.

"I reckon you 'll work now, plague on you!" he exclaimed.

At this juncture Miss Elviry came out, wondering what the children were doing. Watching the manipulations of her brother, she laughed uneasily, saying: "You may thank your stars there ain't no law agin witchcraft in this part of the country. That 's all that keeps 'em from stringin' you up."

"Where 's any witchcraft?" inquired Mr. Bobs indignantly. "I 'm jest a-showin' these youngsters a trick that I larnt from that thar gypsy 'oman — the one that kyored your rheumatiz."

"Well," remarked Miss Elviry, "when folks do somethin' new an' quare, they allers fly back to conjuration to account fer it."

"I don't keer where they fly," said Mr. Bobs, "so long as they don't fly at me."

And, as if to show that he really did n't care, he seized the wooden paddle and began to whip the water again. This time all the bubbles disappeared save one, and the more Mr. Bobs whipped the water the larger it grew. Presently he placed the pan on a large block — the butt-cut of a poplar tree which served sometimes as a table and sometimes as the work-bench — and continued to whip the water, the bubble growing larger and larger all the while. Occasionally he poked his paddle into the bubble and withdrew it quickly, as if to test its consistency. The children could see the paddle go into the bubble and see it come out, but the bubble itself remained intact, and continued to expand.

"You see dat, don't you?" exclaimed Drusilla. The bubble was now as tall as the tallest of the children, and large around in proportion.

Mr. Bobs took his pipe, inserted it in the bubble at the edge of the pan, and began to blow with all his might. This he did at short intervals until all the water in the pan seemed to be exhausted. Then, with the stem of the pipe still in his mouth, he took the paddle and carefully scraped the bubble from the edge of the pan, and by a deft motion of his hand, removed the bubble entirely.

This was certainly a sight for the children to see — a bubble as high and as big as a small house, swaying gently in the sunlight, and showing forth all the colors of the rainbow. It was very wonderful, indeed, and Sweetest Susan was quick to declare that she had never before seen anything so beautiful.

Mr. Bobs seemed to be very much gratified at this. "'T ain't the best I can do," he explained. "I 'd have to make a dozen or more before I got my hand in. But this un is good enough. Ef you find anybody 'round here what can build a bubble that won't bust ner float off, why, jest ax 'em to do it, that 's all. No," he declared, "that ain't all, nuther."

He took a small leaf and laid it on the side of

the bubble. Instantly it began to rotate and travel in a small circle, drawing after it, as it seemed, the most beautiful shades of green, and gold, and purple. It seemed, indeed, to be the centre of an iridescent whirlpool, and the children stood gazing at it with open mouths and eyes.

The glistening colors appealed strongly to Drusilla. "Ef you could hear brass bands a-playin'," she exclaimed, "dis would n't lack much er bein' a whole circus."

Mr. Bobs walked around the bubble and examined it critically, smoothing it with his wooden paddle.

"I 'm jest a-feelin' 'round fer to find whar the door is," he explained. Apparently he soon found it, for he spoke to Buster John. "Come on," he said, "jump right in." The youngster hesitated for an instant, but his surroundings gave him assurance. "Walk right in," Mr. Bobs insisted, and gave a quick flirt with the paddle as Buster John touched the bubble — a quick flirt with the paddle, and Sweetest Susan and Drusilla saw Buster John disappear, swallowed up, as it were, by the bubble.

"Now, then," said Mr. Bobs, waving his paddle

IT WAS VERY WONDERFUL

on high, "come on, an' in wi' you! There, plunge right in!"

Sweetest Susan went forward timidly. "Is it going to fly away with us, Mr. Bobs?" she asked. She had already experienced one adventure that was not pleasing to think of.

"Why, what idees you 've got, honey!" exclaimed Mr. Bobs. "How can a bubble fly away with you children on the inside? You might as well ax me ef a crow can fly away wi' a bale of cotton."

"But this bubble is different from other bubbles," suggested Sweetest Susan.

"It is; it shore is," assented Mr. Bobs; "it shore is, fer I made it myself. But in wi' you; don't let your buddy git lonesome."

Sweetest Susan was still a little afraid, but she went forward all the same, and the bubble seemed to swallow her just as it had swallowed Buster John.

Mr. Bobs now turned to Drusilla. "Come on, ef you 're a-comin'."

"I ain't bleedge ter go in dar, is I?" she asked.

"Go in, or stay out; it 's all one to me. Come!

Talk out! Which is it? It'll do you no good to go in, ner no harm, nuther."

Drusilla hesitated a moment, just a moment, and then she went to the bubble. "I don't want none er dat ar soap-suds ter git in my eyes," she remarked with a shiver.

"Shet your eyes, then," said Mr. Bobs.

Drusilla did more than that; she held her breath. Then, with a whiff of dampness on her face, she found herself inside the bubble. She turned to see where and how she had come in, but she was so surprised at the view that presented itself, that she fairly gasped with astonishment. Away off in the distance she could see somebody that resembled Mr. Bobs, but he seemed to be hanging in the air, heels upward. Not far from him was his house; and that, too, was upside down. By some curious freak of perspective, the house and its surroundings, including Mr. Bobs, presented a picture not larger than your thumbnail.

"I did n't know I wuz sech a mighty jumper," said Drusilla to herself.

Then she looked around for Buster John and Sweetest Susan, and saw them some distance away. They were evidently as much puzzled as she was.

The bubble no longer seemed to be a bubble. Viewed from the outside, it had appeared to be no larger than a small house. In the inside, however, as Drusilla remarked, it was as big as all outdoors. They walked about timidly at first, for fear of breaking the bubble, but they soon forgot all about their precaution. They seemed to be in a wide and perfectly level field — a field with a shining floor. Over this floor the many-hued colors of the rainbow chased one another incessantly, wriggling, twisting, whirling. The children watched this display until Drusilla made a remark that had astonishing results.

"I know whar we at," she said; "dish yer place is whar dey make rainbows. You kin see um plattin' um now."

At this both Buster John and Sweetest Susan laughed aloud; whereupon the rainbow colors seemed to be shattered into thousands of fragments, and they ran about on the floor, shaken into all sorts of disturbed states. Almost as curious as this spectacle were the wonderful echoes that took up the sound of the children's laughter, carrying it away and bringing it back again in a greater volume. A thousand children seemed to be laughing, sometimes close at hand, and then far away.

Drusilla was alarmed. "I done tol' you-all 'bout puttin' yo' heads in all kinder holes an' traps," she said under her breath. "You may call dis a bubble ef you wanter; but 't ain't no mo' a bubble dan I 'm a bubble. Look over yo' head; does you see any bubble-skin, er frame, er hide, er whatsomever you may call it? No, you don't. 'Stidder dat, you see two suns a-shinin'. I done promise myse'f when we went und' dat spring dat I wa'n't gwine ter let you drag me in no mo' places. An' yit, here I is! You done drag me in here, an' now you got ter drag me out — ef I ever is ter git out."

"Why, there 's nothing to do but to break the bubble," Buster John stoutly asserted.

"Show me whar dey 's any bubble," cried Drusilla. "You don't see none, an' I don't see none. We 're in a rainbow fact'ry, an' we better git out fo' it thunders."

Drusilla's considerations led the children to look around them more carefully than they had done; and even Buster John was compelled to admit that he could see nothing like the walls of a bubble, if walls they may be called.

One fact that disturbed them more than any other, was that they could see no horizon line. The horizon exists only in the imagination, but it plays a very important part in our actual experience. It provides a boundary, a limit. But it was absent now, and its absence, together with the fact that two separate and distinct suns appeared to be shining overhead, gave a weird aspect to this new landscape, or, to be more exact, the bubble-scape. And while the shimmering, seething, whirling, rainbow colors were beautiful to behold, they began to add to the confusion after a while.

In the midst of it all, Drusilla sneezed, not once, but twice. She tried hard to keep the sneezes back, to "hol' um in," as she said, but they had to come, and when they did come, they seemed to shake the foundation of things, and the sound of ten thousand sneezes was heard in the air. The two suns overhead reeled and shook and whirled about each other, and the colors whirled in the floor till they lost all semblance of proportion.

And then, while waiting for this devastation to stop itself, the children saw a little woman come gliding toward them, followed by a swarm of smaller figures.

"We 're gone now!" exclaimed Drusilla excitedly. "We done stirred um up. We better make a break an' git out er here 'fo' dey jump on us an' git us down."

But somehow, neither Buster John nor Sweetest Susan was frightened. There was nothing alarming about these little people — if people they were. The little woman, who seemed to be the leader, was not ugly at all. If she had been an old crone with a yellow tooth, the children might have felt some uneasiness, but her appearance was very pleasing, although she seemed to be somewhat weary. And all the smaller ones that came after her seemed to be solemn and weary. But they were not too weary to form themselves in a ring, of which the children were the centre, and go marching around, singing a song of complaint. Their voices were not strong, and it was all the children could do to catch a few of the words of the song. A part of it was as follows: —

"If you stay awake while you sleep,
You will find that the whole is n't half:
You will find it is funny to weep,
And awfully solemn to laugh.

Oh, hear our cause of complaint —
It 't is, it 't was, and it 't ain't!"

"I tell you dey got us!" said Drusilla in a low tone. "Dey ain't no sense in what dey singin'. Dey er all ravin' crazy. Look at um, how dey waggle der heads an' wobble 'bout when dey walk! Dey sho is got us!"

When the song, if such it could be called, was done, the little woman came towards the children. Her attitude was not threatening, but Drusilla made haste to get behind her companions.

"You don't seem to know me," the little woman said.

"No, we don't. Who are you?" asked Sweetest Susan.

"I 'm the Queen of Dreams," replied the other.

"Are we dreaming now?" Buster John asked somewhat bluntly.

"How could that be?" said the Queen of Dreams. "You are not asleep; and we are only here because of a hideous noise we heard. We were asleep. Do you think we should be disturbed in our own kingdom? We can't help ourselves at this moment, but do you think it is right to invade our territory?"

"What she talkin' 'bout?" asked Drusilla in a whisper. "Who been 'vadin' any ter'ytory?"

"Why, Mr. Bobs made this bubble for us," Buster John explained.

The Queen of Dreams seemed to be puzzled. "What is a bubble?" she asked.

"Why, a bubble — a bubble is — well, a bubble is a piece of soap-suds into which air has been blown," replied Sweetest Susan, somewhat doubtfully.

"How big a piece, and how much air is necessary to make a bubble?" inquired the Queen of Dreams.

"I'm sure I don't know," responded Sweetest Susan. "Bubbles are of all sizes; but this one is the largest I ever saw."

"Which one?" The Queen of Dreams was a very persistent seeker after information.

"The bubble we are in now," explained Sweetest Susan.

The Queen of Dreams shook her head and frowned slightly. At this Drusilla nudged Buster John, and remarked in a whisper: "I done tol' you we ain't got no business in here — ef we is in here. Dem ar creeturs 'll sho do us damage."

But the Queen of Dreams was not angry; she was only puzzled. In a little while she tried to make herself very pleasant. She seemed to be very proud of her subjects. She paraded them before the children, and called off their names. There were Mince Pie Dream, and his twin brother, Fruit Cake Dream, and Muffin and Waffles, and Green Apple Dreams, and ever so many more. While the Queen of Dreams was describing the beauties of her dyspeptic subjects, Drusilla saw coming toward them the most horrible-looking object imaginable. She tried to warn the others, but she could n't speak. She could only point her finger and nod her head. The creature seemed to be as big around the body as a horse. Its forelegs were short, while its hind legs were long, so that in crawling along the ground as it was now doing, it seemed to be crouching as if ready to spring. It had two tails longer than an alligator's body, and its head was as big as a barrel and shaped something like that of a hippopotamus. But its ears were long as those of a mule; its eyes were large and green, and, when it gaped, the inside of its mouth was as red as red flannel.

Seeing the children huddled together in a stupefying fright, the Queen of Dreams told them they had nothing to fear. "It 's nobody but poor old Nightmare. He was out all last night, and worked hard at his business. He should be resting now, but the poor thing gets lonely when he opens one eye and finds us gone. He 's a great pet of mine. Come, tickle his ear, and see him open his mouth and growl."

At this Drusilla turned and ran, and the children after her, and the next moment they were standing, panting for breath, close to Mr. Bobs, who was calmly sharpening his tools on an oil stone.

"I clean forgot to tell you not to stay in there too long," he remarked. "Folks must have fresh air, and you can't git that in a bubble. But ef you say the word, I 'll blow you up a bigger one, and you can stay in it longer."

But the children shook their heads and thanked him. They did n't want any more bubbles that day.

"You better le' me make you a good big un," Mr. Bobs insisted. "I 'most know the nigger gal there would like to git in a great big un."

DRUSILLA TURNED AND RAN, AND THE CHILDREN AFTER HER

"Humph! You don't know me, den," said Drusilla with some bluntness. "Dem what likes bubbles can git in um an' stay in um fer what I keer. All I 'm skeered un is dat I 'll git in um in my dreams. Ef I does, eve'y hair in my haid 'll be gray de nex' time you see me."

At this Mr. Bobs fell to laughing, and he laughed so long and so loudly that Miss Elviry came to the door to see what the matter was.

"Why, what in the world!" she exclaimed.

"I 'm jest laughin' at that gal there," Mr. Bobs explained, when he could control himself. "She went into the bubble along wi' the others."

"Why will you go on that away? An' at your age, too. It 's a plum' shame!" exclaimed his sister.

"Why, Elviry, ten year from now these youngsters would n't take a hundred dollars for what they 've saw to-day."

And no doubt this was true, so far as Buster John and Sweetest Susan were concerned; but with Drusilla it was different. For many months she was filled with indignation toward Mr. Bobs, and it was many months more before she could be induced to go out of the house alone at night.

Even then she would say, "Ef you want me ter go, you better gi' me a bottle er some kinder med'cine, kaze ef I meet dat Thing out dar, I'll have ten fits 'fo' you kin ax me what de matter."

If the children were not willing to say that Mr. Bobs was a smarter man than Aaron, they were, at any rate, willing to admit that he had given them something to talk about. Drusilla, however, refused to admit that there was any merit in that.

"Ef dat ol' white man 'll gi' me sump'n dat 'll wipe all dat out 'n my min' an' make me fergit 'bout him an' his bubble, I 'll say anywhar dat he de smartest man in de worl'; but whar is dey any smartness in skeerin' chillun out'n der growth? Ez I is now, des so you 'll see me when I 'm seventy year ol'. Ef gittin' skeer'd 'll stunt folks, den I 'm done stunted, an' stunted bad."

"Maybe we were dreaming," Sweetest Susan suggested when Drusilla made this remark.

"Dream nothin'!" Drusilla retorted. "How kin folks stan' flat-footed in de broad open daylight, an' have 'zactly de same dream? Nobody ain't never see no creetur like dat, in no dream, kaze ef dey did, folks ud set up an' hire somebody fer ter keep um 'wake. You-all do mighty funny. Wuz you too skeered ter look at de cree-tur? Here's what uz des skeer'd 'nough ter look at it good. You call dat dreamin', does you?"

The truth is, the whole affair had been so unusual, so unexpected and unique, that it took its place in Sweetest Susan's mind, as well as in Buster John's, as a sort of waking dream. But Drusilla had seen what she had seen, and to use her own expression, she had looked at it mighty hard.

Buster John and Sweetest Susan were very shy in telling their experiences in the bubble to their elders. They had been laughed at on other occa-sions when giving hints as to what they had seen in the country next door to the world, and that fact made them somewhat doubtful and timid. As for Drusilla, she had in the negroes an audi-ence ready to welcome any statement, no matter how wonderful. Words were unable to convey to their minds a real comprehension of what Drusilla had seen, but they knew it was some-thing awful, and from that time forward they and all the negroes for miles around regarded Mr.

Bobs and his sister as conjurers in active practice. In a way, this notoriety helped Mr. Bobs, for no negro refused to work for him when requested. But no negro would remain near his house at night. This, however, did not grieve him to any great extent.

VII.

A TALK ABOUT FOX HUNTING.

In the South, December is usually marked by very fair weather, the mornings cool and crisp, and the afternoons warm and balmy enough to invite the mocking-birds to sing. The December following Sherman's march to the sea was no exception, and as the holiday season drew near, Buster John and Sweetest Susan heard hints to the effect that some of their grandfather's kinsmen and friends intended to assemble at the Abercrombie place and indulge in an old-fashioned fox hunt. It might be thought that all the able-bodied men of the region were fighting; but war is never so exacting that it sweeps everybody into the ranks, and there were many men exempted from conscription either by their occupation or by their age.

The news of the fox hunt was not particularly interesting to Sweetest Susan, but Buster John was stirred by it. He wondered why it was that he should be too young to go fox hunting; and the more he thought about it, the stronger grew the conviction that youth is a hardship invented to punish children. His views in that respect underwent a great change some years later, but at that particular time, he was quite sure that youth was something that had to be endured, only because there was no help for it. His mind was full of fox hunting, and he sought information on the matter whenever it was to be found. Old Fountain was an authority on the subject, so Buster John was told, and the youngster lost no time in questioning the negro.

"Uncle Fountain," he said on the first occasion that presented itself, "they say there 's going to be a big fox hunt here Christmas week."

"I hear um sesso," replied Fountain. "Well, let um hunt ef dey will; I done had my day at dat, I 'speck. Dey use ter hunt fum here a right smart; an' when dey got in de notion, nobody could n't do nothin' fer um but Fountain. 'T wuz 'Fountain' here and 'Fountain' dar, twel some er de quality, new ter de place, would up an' ax ef all de niggers on de plantation is name Fountain. Yes — yes, suh — I see myse'f now havin' de mommuck made fer de dogs, corn meal stewed thick, wid a han'ful er cracklin's flung in; an' den de nex' mornin', 'fo' day, de cry would be fer Fountain; an' nothin' would do, but Fountain mus' straddle a mule — ol' Puss, de pacin' mule — an' go 'long wid um. I had lim's in dem days, an' lungs, ef you 'll believe me. Yes — yes, suh — I wuz soople fum de word go — work all day, an' frolic all night."

"Dat 's so," said Big Sal, lifting her sad face and looking at the children.

"I 'member one time," Fountain continued, "dat I went 'long fer ter look atter de Little Marster" — he paused and began to pick at a patched place on his knee, and Big Sal drew a long breath. "Now, dar wuz a chap fer you!" he exclaimed enthusiastically. "Dey say he died kaze he wuz puny; but don't you b'lieve it; he died kaze his heart an' his head wuz too big. Dey tuck in all dat he yever seed, er heard, er dre'mpt 'bout. No human bein' could go thoo life wid dat kinder head an' heart; it 's agin' natur'."

"Dat 's de Lord's trufe!" cried Big Sal.

The children knew, of course, that the reference was to Little Crotchet, dead long ago, and so they sat silent and thoughtful.

"Yes—yes, suh—I 'member de time des ez well es ef 't wuz yistiddy, maybe better. We put out, we did, 'bout light; an' 'fo' we went a mile up jumped a gray—de reds had n't come in den—an' here dey had it 'roun' an' 'roun' same ez chasin' a rabbit. I wuz ter take keer er de Little Marster, but bless yo' soul! he ain't gi' me time ter do dat. I allers shill b'lieve dat him an' dat gray pony had some deep pardnership wid one anudder, bekaze ef it had n't been fer dat, de Little Marster would 'a' been drug out de saddle whilst dey runnin' thoo de scrub pines an' de black jacks. Dey went skeetin' here an' dar, an' when de dogs ketched, dar wuz de Little Marster, an' de pony, right in 'mongst um. Hit 's so, ez sho ez I 'm a-settin' here."

Fountain paused and sighed, then he went on: "I 'speck my blood 'll be het up ef I hear de horn a-blowin' and de dogs a-yelpin', but I 'm lots too old fer dem kinder doin's. Let um call on Johnny Bapter. He may not be so mighty knowin', but he 's young and soople. But in times now gone, mo' speshually when de reds come in an' driv' de grays out, I know'd de feedin' groun' an' de promenade of all de foxes fum here ter de river — eve'y one un um. An' mo' dan dat, I know whar one ol' red stays right now. He 's ez big ez a cur dog. Folks tried de'r level bes' fer ter ketch dat ol' fox 'fo' de war. Dey brung dogs here fum away off yan', but he des played wid um. He kin tell a houn' fum a house dog by de bark, an' time he hear one atter midnight, he done gone — he done up an' gone! He got a white patch 'twixt his eyes, an' on 'count er dat, day call 'im Scour-Face."

"Scar-Face," Buster John corrected. "Why, he 's the fox they are going to catch!"

Fountain laughed softly. "Oh, dey er gwine ter ketch 'im? Well, atter he 's cotch, I hope dey 'll show im ter me. Scour-Face, er Scyar-Face, I wanter see what dat white mark is 'twixt his eyes."

"They are going to bring Birdsong dogs," explained Buster John.

"Well, dey 'll hatter sing bird song er some yuther kinder song 'fo' dey ketch dat fox."

"Besides all the other dogs, Joe Maxwell is to bring Hodo," remarked Buster John.

"I hear tell er dat dog," replied Fountain. "Dey say he sho is a mover. But, shucks! you kin hear dat kinder talk about mos' any dog. But dish yer Hoodo got ter have brains ez well as legs ef he ketch ol' Scour-Face. I 'm a-talkin' now, sho."

"Where does old Scar-Face stay, Uncle Fountain?" asked Buster John.

"You know dat ar broom-sage fiel' right up yan', cross de road fum de gin-house? Well, he stay right dar. Ef you wuz ter go out er de door dar an' holler right loud, he 'd hear you, less'n he 's promenadin' some'rs else. He been dar dis long time. Dey don't a week pass but what I sees him slippin' an' slidin' 'long. He moves des like a shadder; once an' awhile he 'll stop an' look at you, but mos' er de time it 's fwiff! an' he done gone. He got sense same ez folks."

Buster John asked Fountain a great many questions about Scar-Face, with the result that he made up his mind to see the fox himself. His curiosity affected Sweetest Susan, and she expressed a desire to see old Scar-Face. As for

Drusilla, she did n't care one way or the other. So long as there was no bubble and no live nightmares around, she was satisfied — at least, she was not contentious; though she predicted now, as she had been predicting all along, that the children would "keep on foolin' 'roun' an' gwine whar dey got no business twel some kind er creetur would snap um up, an' walk off wid um."

It was an easy matter for Buster John and Sweetest Susan to say they would like to see old Scar-Face, the Red Fox, but how to see him was a very different matter. They might walk through the "broom-sage" every day for a week, or a month, or a year, and never see him; they might sit in the fence corner and peep between the rails from sun-up till sun-down, and never catch a glimpse of him. Old Scar-Face would see them. Oh, yes! no doubt about that. It was his business to see without being seen. He began to learn that trade when he was n't bigger than Buster John's two fists; and by constant practice he had developed it into a fine art. The shyest and wariest birds could light within an inch of his nose and never see him; could light there, but they never flew away any more. Old Molly

to fox, the reds can whip the grays, and this fact has become so well established that the grays always get out of the way when they can. It happened one day, when Scar-Face was a "puppy," as Aaron said, with big legs and a very wobbly body, he met a big gray in the woods. Some instinct or other caused the red to rush at the gray, and that was the cause of the red's scar. The gray would have run away if he could, but Scar-Face caught him by the flank and held on like a bull-terrier, while the gray, frightened and hurt, gnawed away on Scar-Face's head until the top of it was bare of hide and hair.

It was then that the Son of Ben Ali chanced to pass, and the gray with a scream of fear tore away, leaving some of his pelt between Scar-Face's teeth. After some trouble, Aaron explained to the red that he was no enemy, having himself been a hunted animal at one time. He "doctored" the torn head the best he could, but the wound left a mark, a bare place fringed with white hair.

Aaron was very much interested in the proposed fox hunt, and asked many questions about it. Finally he promised the children that, if they would remind him of it the next afternoon, he would go with them to the sedge-field and try to find old Scar-Face. He counted on his fingers, and made out the age of the red to be nearly eight years, and concluded that if the dogs were good and swift, they ought to be able to run him down in about eight hours.

"If 't was me," remarked the Son of Ben Ali, "I 'd find out the day the dogs come, and then I 'd pack my wallet, and take my walking-stick, and move into the middle of the big swamp. But he won't do it. He don't like the swamp; too much water, maybe, or maybe too much coon. I 'll give him fair warning."

The next afternoon being clear and pleasant, the children were trotting to Aaron's heels a full hour before he was ready to go. If he had to go to the horse-lot, they trotted after him; if to the carriage house, it was the same thing. Occupied with so many duties, he sometimes forgot his half playful promises, and so, when the youngsters were in earnest about anything, they had a habit of trotting at his heels until, in sheer self-defense, he was compelled to carry out their wishes as far as he could. Toward the middle of the afternoon he announced himself ready, and, with Buster John and Sweetest Susan jumping and skipping at his side, and Drusilla more soberly bringing up the rear, he went to the field where old Scar-Face was said to have his home. Before the broom-sedge took it, the field had been used as a pasture for the cows, but it was now pastured only in the early spring, when the tender shoots of the sedge are putting out. This was why bars took the place of a gate. Two of the bars were already down, and it was an easy matter for the Son of Ben Ali to stoop and pass under the topmost bar. The children following promptly, he paused to arrange the entrance so that no stray cattle from neighboring plantations might wander in. Aaron's caution was simply the result of the force of habit. The Federal army had spared the stock on the Abercrombie place as we have seen, but there were few cattle left in all that region to stray through open gates or fallen bars.

"We are hunting foxes on a new plan," said Buster somewhat boastfully. But Aaron warned him to be quiet.

They went through the sedge, which was as

high as Aaron's waist, and higher than Sweetest Susan's head, until they came to a pine thicket. In a desert this small pine orchard would be called an oasis. In the sedge-field it was known as the pine thicket. The pines were not large; they had sprung up since the field had been abandoned; but they were large enough and thick enough to afford shelter from the sun in hot weather, and to form a sort of playground or meeting place for the wild creatures at night. On the side toward the high road, the sedge shut this playground in from observation, and on the opposite side there was a wall of brambles and wild briars and blackberry bushes.

This wall had a door, too. When the rains fell, the lay of the land caused hundreds of little rivulets to trickle through the sedge toward the thicket. On the other side, these tiny rivulets coming together gathered force and strength, and the force thus collected dug its way through the briary wall. By some this door would be called a drain or "dreen," by others, a gully. Anyhow, there it was, and in good weather it formed a neat entrance for the wild creatures coming from the forest side.

It was to this playground that Aaron led the youngsters. By a motion of his hand, the Son of Ben Ali indicated that they were to sit on the carpet of pine needles, thickly spread over the ground. He had no need to ask them to refrain from talking. His expectant attitude was sufficient of itself to command their silence, and there was something in the situation that kept the children quiet. They felt now, as they sometimes did when playing hide and seek in the big, dark barn, when those who played the part of It were afraid that one of the hidden ones, or something else, would jump out of the gloom and seize them.

Aaron remained standing, one hand resting on the trunk of a pine. The silence was so profound that the wind softly blowing through the dry sedge sounded like the flight of frightened creatures. How long they remained thus, the children could never guess, but it seemed a very long time indeed. Suddenly, the Son of Ben Ali, using his hand as a sort of trumpet, gave a peculiar cry, which was thrice repeated. The children having been "touched" understood this at once.

"I AM HERE, SON OF BEN ALI"

VIII.

OLD SCAR-FACE, THE RED FOX, DOES SOME BRAGGING.

"WHAT is it, and who is it?" old Scar-Face repeated, holding himself ready to disappear in the bushes at a word, or a motion of the hand. But the children had had some experience with wild creatures, and they sat as still as statues.

"The time was," said the Son of Ben Ali, "when you came at my call and asked no questions. You have forgotten, but I remember."

"No, Son of Ben Ali," old Scar-Face replied, "I have not forgotten; but when you came, you came alone; you brought no strangers with you."

"I said you had forgotten," remarked Aaron. "What of Rambler, the track-dog?"

"True! Oh, most true, Son of Ben Ali!" exclaimed old Scar-Face, lowering his head in apparent humility, a fact that caused Drusilla to remark, in a whisper, "He do like he human!"

And the countenance of old Scar-Face, cruel and crafty, certainly had a human aspect. The children tried in vain to remember whom he resembled. One and all were sure in their own minds they had seen some one who looked like him. Here was the personification of craft and fear — the sharp nose, the white teeth gleaming, the glittering, shifty eyes, the pointed ears turning about to catch every sound, and so keen of hearing that the fall of a pine needle attracted their attention.

This was old Scar-Face the invincible, celebrated throughout Middle Georgia as the fox which had out-footed, and out-manœuvred every kennel of hounds brought against him. The ordinary hounds which had been used for chasing gray foxes were simply the playthings of old Scar-Face. It was his pleasure to use them for the purpose of practicing new movements. He had one scheme, which, when he was not feeling well, he was in the habit of working on his pursuers. It may be called the triple loops, each loop being a mile or a half-mile in circumference, the extent depending on circumstances. Here is a diagram of the movement: —

Imagine the loops to cover a half-mile each, and the difficulty which a dog would have in untangling them with his nose, and that, too, while he is trying to go at full speed, will be easily perceived. When the ordinary hounds failed to catch old Scar-Face, hunters from a distance came with their Birdsong hounds. These were Irish dogs, but were called Birdsong because they were first bred in Georgia by a planter of that name. These taught old Scar-Face the necessity of getting on foot whenever he heard a hound bark between midnight and day; but when the Birdsong hounds found his drag warm, the triple loops were sufficient to throw them out.

Here, then was this famous old fox, grinning at Aaron and the children, almost within reach of their hands. Sweetest Susan and Drusilla were plainly afraid of him, for the white scar on his forehead did not add to his beauty; but Buster John regarded him with great curiosity and interest.

"I had forgotten Rambler, Son of Ben Ali," said old Scar-Face musingly. "But I was not the first to forget; more than once I heard Rambler howling for my blood."

"Yes; he made no bargain with me," Aaron remarked. "But here are those who have heard of you, and who begged to see you. They have some news for you."

"It is long since I had any," said old Scar-Face.

Whereupon Aaron told of the fox hunt that was to take place, and of a hound named Hodo, who was almost as famous among fox-hunters as old Scar-Face himself. During this recital the fox came out of the tunnel, but sat upon his haunches close to the mouth of it, and held himself in readiness to take refuge therein on the slightest alarm.

"When is the hunt to be?" asked old Scar-Face.

"In the days when there is no working in the fields and woods. When you fail to hear the axe

READY TO DISAPPEAR IN THE BUSHES

and the rattle of the wagon, then you may know the time for the hunt is near at hand," said Aaron.

There was a pause, and during this pause a hare, a small, palpitating creature, came creeping from the sedge and sat looking at Aaron and the children. Some movement or other frightened it, and it bounded away. Old Scar-Face disappeared in the tunnel like a shadow, and presently those who were listening heard the poor little hare give one scream of agony and fright, and then all was still.

"What hurt the rabbit?" asked Sweetest Susan. "I think it 's a shame," she cried, when Aaron motioned with his hand to indicate the fox. As she spoke, old Scar-Face appeared at the door of the tunnel. At his feet lay the rabbit.

Sweetest Susan looked appealingly at Aaron; but appealing looks could n't bring the hare back to life.

"I feel better," remarked old Scar-Face, licking his chops. "I have n't had a good dinner in two suns. They are hard to catch."

"You are getting old," suggested Aaron.

"Yes, old; but I gave this little creature a fair chance."

"It was a quick catch," Aaron declared.

"Neat, if not quick," said old Scar-Face, with an air of pride. "I'm old, but not too old for this — not too old to lead into the middle winds this great dog you tell of."

"What are the 'middle winds?'" Buster John asked in a whisper.

"Where there is no scent," Aaron explained.

"There is scent enough," remarked old Scar-Face, "but it is lifted from ground and grass by the winds. Yes, I will lead this wonderful dog into the middle winds, and leave him there; or I will carry him to the barren places where the ground is red and dry, or where the sand has drifted. It is now three years since I have done more than trot before the dogs they bring. What I need, Son of Ben Ali, is something to stir the blood and make me thirsty."

"This dog they will bring will give you what you want," said Aaron. "He is called Hodo."

"What is that, Son of Ben Ali?"

"It is his name."

"Well, my name is Woodranger. What do your kind call me, Son of Ben Ali?"

"Scar-Face," replied Aaron bluntly.

"It is as good as any," said the fox.

"Yes, one name is as good as another when you have three meals a day," Aaron assented.

"There was a time," suggested old Scar-Face, "when the Son of Ben Ali killed and brought me birds; but that time is past."

"You are no longer weak and young. But I came to-day to do you a better turn than that. I came to warn you of this dog from a strange settlement, whose nose is so keen that he never puts it to the ground, and whose legs are so strong that he but touches the top of a ten-rail fence as he goes over. Take my word for it; let not another sun rise on you here till the grass is green again. Go to the river; hide in the big swamp; stay anywhere but here. Let the dog with the queer name run down and kill one of your brethren. Do you move away for a time and go where the hunters may not follow."

Old Scar-Face tried to reach with his hind foot a flea that was tickling him on the top of his back near his shoulder, and in making the effort he stretched out his neck, closed his eye, and grinned so comically that the children laughed.

"Come; I'll scratch you," said Aaron.

Old Scar-Face took a step forward, but hesitated. "No, Son of Ben Ali," he said. "It makes me cold to be too near the new ones."

Whereupon Aaron himself took a step forward and scratched old Scar-Face on the back with a pine cone, and this operation seemed to be so pleasing that the fox kept time to the scratching by patting the ground with one of his hind feet, as though he were trying in this way to aid Aaron. When old Scar-Face had been thoroughly scratched along the spine, where his hind foot could not reach, he shook himself, licked his chops, and seemed to feel very much better.

"And so you think I should move away from my home, Son of Ben Ali," old Scar-Face remarked. "Well, if you had come saying, 'My friend, you are in danger; fly and remain away many suns,' to-morrow's dawn would have found me miles away. But when you say, 'Beware of the dogs; there is one called Hodo coming to run you down,' that is different. I want to hear this strange dog yelping behind me, not too close, but far enough away to make him weary. I want to hear the noise of his yelp, or know that he is running wildly hither and yonder, sick to know where the Woodranger has gone."

"As you please, old friend," said Aaron. "This Hodo has made great talk amongst the hunters. I have warned you; it is all I can do."

"There have been swift dogs after me, Son of Ben Ali; but they have always been behind me. Not one of them has ever untangled the loops of my tangle; not one have I ever carried into the middle winds. This strange dog I should like to carry there if he has strength enough; once there, I 'll bid him good-by."

"You 'll be surprised if he tells you howdy," suggested Aaron.

"So would you, Son of Ben Ali."

"No, you 're wrong; it would be no surprise to me," Aaron replied. "You have won many a race; you have broken down many a pack of hounds; but you are not as young as you were. And something tells me that if you were in your prime, this hound would outfoot you. I know what I know."

"And I know what I can do, Son of Ben Ali; and I 'll show you when the time comes. I 'll give this hound a warm scent, and I 'll cut out for him a journey he 'll long remember."

"This thing of remembering," said Aaron,

"depends on whether you are well enough to remember. I hope you 'll be well enough for that when the race is over."

"Don't worry about me, Son of Ben Ali. Many of the things I know you taught me; many I learned myself. I have been putting them all together until now I want to see what the strange hound will make of them."

"Well, so long," said Aaron. "You are warned; that is enough. Go to your rabbit before it is cold, and I 'll go to my work."

Old Scar-Face disappeared in the tunnel, and Aaron and the children went home.

"Why did you warn him?" Buster John asked, when they were out of the sedge-field.

"Old times — old times," replied Aaron. "When he was a puppy I doctored him, and he used to trot after me in the woods. Now my mind 's easy. If he is caught, well; if he ain't, good. He 's outrun hounds so long that he 's got it in his head that none can catch him. That 's his business."

"I did n't like his looks," said Sweetest Susan after awhile.

"Ner me, needer," Drusilla exclaimed. "He

look too much like folks when he helt his head on one side an' grin. He looked mighty 'umble-come-tumble, when he was settin' dar hangin' his head down, an' talkin' 'bout how he gwine do. You see how he catch dat rabbit? 't was des like snappin' yo' fingers. Dat creetur sho is got de Ol' Boy in 'im. I hope dey 'll ketch 'im."

Buster John said nothing. He was wondering how he could manage to get permission to go on the hunt that had been arranged for. At last he asked Aaron's advice.

"Ride behind some of 'em," Aaron replied.

"Fountain or Johnny Bapter can take one of the carriage horses," Buster John suggested. Aaron nodded his head, and the youngster made up his mind to go with the hunters, unless everybody in the house shut their ears to his pleadings.

Now, Sweetest Susan, who knew that she could not go in any event, was very anxious for her brother to see the hunt, and if her reason was partly a selfish one, it was not different in that respect from the reasons of a great many grown persons. She wanted to hear all about the chase, and she knew that Buster John could tell her about it better than any one else. This was the selfish part.

On the other hand, she also wanted Buster John to go because his desire was so keen. He had never seen a fox hunt, and he was getting quite old enough, in Sweetest Susan's opinion, to share in some of the amusements of his elders. True, fox hunting is a rough sport when it is carried out with energy, but Buster John did n't have to break his neck riding across ditches and gullies, and jumping fences. He could ride behind Fountain or Johnny Bapter, or on one of the fat and sober carriage horses. Sweetest Susan had heard her grandfather say many times that with good dogs, and a hot drag, a fox-hunter need n't ride very far nor very fast to see pretty much all there is to be seen of a fox hunt. She did n't remember just these words, but she knew what her grandfather meant, for he himself was among those who ceased to be ambitious to "tail the fox," and was content to canter from one position to another, so as to be able to see the most exciting events in a fox chase.

So the youngsters, as children will, put their heads together and laid the plan of a campaign, and it was a very cunning one, too. Not a word was to be said about the hunt until they knew the very day on which it was to take place. Then the day before, the matter was to be broached by Jemimy, not seriously, but in a half-joking way. This would be followed by Sweetest Susan, and then Buster John himself would make an appeal, an appeal full of tears if necessary.

"You never have seen me cry as hard as I can," he declared to Sweetest Susan.

"What you wanter wait so long 'fo' you git atter um 'bout it?" inquired Drusilla.

"Yes," said Sweetest Susan, "why?"

"If you begin too soon," explained Buster John, "mamma will find forty reasons why I should n't go, and they 'll all be good ones. If we begin the day before, she 'll be too busy fixing up the house for the gentlemen who are to go hunting; she 'll be too busy to find any reasons. You know how mamma is when company is coming."

"I 'm dreadin' de day," said Drusilla with emphasis. "When comp'ny comin', de whole house got ter be tore up an' cleaned, and eve'ything got ter be desso."

"And when company comes," chimed in Sweetest Susan, "she 'll let us do anything we ask her, almost. When Mrs. Terrell came that time, I asked mamma if me and Drusilla might play in the barn loft, and she kissed me and said 'yes.' And the next day she happened to think about the loose planks up there, and then she said we must n't go in the loft never any more."

"If Mrs. Terrell had n't been there," said Buster John, "she 'd have thought about the loose planks right on the spot." And to this Sweetest Susan readily assented.

Their mother, like most mothers, had not the faintest idea that the children were able to put their small fingers on some of her characteristics; but youngsters the world over are more observing and know a great deal more than their elders give them credit for. The most of them are discreet enough to keep their knowledge to themselves.

Well, Buster John's plan of campaign was as we have outlined above, and (though he did afterwards develop into a very successful politician) it must not be supposed that his plan displayed any special aptness or brilliancy. No, he was merely a very bright boy, whose common sense was in process of development.

Moreover, if his plan had cost him any serious thought, it would have been labor thrown away; for as matters turned out, it was not necessary at all. Indeed, it might have failed, but for one of those lucky incidents that sometimes happen to us all. Buster John not only saw the fox hunt, or at least the part of it that could be seen, but he saw it in such a fortunate way, and under such delightful circumstances, that it remained for many years a red-letter day in his memory.

IX.

BUSTER JOHN SEES HODO.

Now the lucky chance which gave Buster John opportunity to see the fox hunt was both curious and interesting. The date was fixed upon, and the children's grandfather invited the hunters to spend the night with him, so as to have an early start the next morning. So, one Friday afternoon — the hunt was to take place on Saturday — the hunters began to arrive, some singly and some in couples, until all had arrived except young Maxwell and his hound Hodo. Mr. Kilpatrick came, bringing Music and Whalebone and Tip, with others. Mr. Collingsworth brought Fanny and Rocket and Bartow, with their chorus; and Mr. Dennis brought Rowan and Ruth and Top and Flirt. There were other hunters with their dogs, and one or two gentlemen who had no dogs, but who wanted to see the sport.

But these hunters, their friends, and their dogs,

were not the ones Buster John wanted to see. So he continued to watch the big gate at the head of the avenue. Sweetest Susan watched with him, Drusilla being busy helping their mother, who, as a good housekeeper, looked after her dining-room and was not afraid to go into the kitchen. Buster John was anxious lest young Maxwell would fail to come, and said so many times. He had once heard his grandfather reading something that Maxwell had written in the county paper, and he had also heard the negroes talking about the young man, how clever and kind he was. And then his horse, Butterfly, and his hound, Hodo! What wonderful tales old Fountain and Johnny Bapter had told about these animals!

But when the sun was about an hour high, and just as Buster John had given up all hope, he saw the big gate swing open. A large dog came through, and after him a rider on a sorrel horse. Without alighting from his horse, the rider pulled the gate to, and, leaning down until Buster John could see nothing but one of his feet pressing against the saddle, fastened the catch. Buster John had never seen the gate opened and shut in this fashion before, for the latch had been pur-

While he was speaking, Johnny Bapter pushed the children around deftly so that they exchanged positions.

Then, "I'll take de bet!" exclaimed Johnny Bapter.

"You've lost," said young Maxwell; "look at my hand." It was open; the forefinger was pointing at Buster John, and the little finger at Sweetest Susan.

This sort of an introduction charmed the children, who were shy, and put them at their ease at once.

"Here's your tobacco, Johnny Bapter. Now don't feed my horse till I come out to-night, and do put him in a dry place where the wind can't strike him, and if you have time wash his legs. The roads are awful. Hang my saddle and blanket on the side fence yonder. I'll go in and tell 'em howdy, and then I'll come out and look after things."

He went in the house with each of the children holding him by a hand. He seemed to be a child with them. He shook hands with the host and with the other guests, and excused himself on the plea that he wanted to have a frolic with the children. He was seventeen, but had none of the characteristics of that age. He was even more juvenile in his actions than Sweetest Susan. He made the children call him Joe, and asked them if there was a shelter where he could put his saddle to keep it out of the dew.

"Make Johnny Bapter hang it up with the rest in the carriage house," suggested Buster John.

"No," said young Maxwell. "This is a peculiar saddle. It has a dog tied to it by an invisible string." Sure enough! When they reached the side fence, there was Hodo lying directly under the saddle and blanket, which Johnny Bapter had placed on the fence. "You can see the dog and saddle," remarked Maxwell, "but you can't see the string."

Buster John suggested the old carpenter shop, a long shed room, the entrance to which had no door. There was a pile of shavings in the shop, and Joe Maxwell said it was the very place of all others. So he placed his saddle on the workbench, kicked the shavings together, and told Hodo he could go to bed and pull the cover over his head when he got ready.

"Will he stay?" Buster John asked.

The other dogs were all fastened up in the blacksmith shop to keep them from going home.

Young Maxwell laughed. "He 'll stay there till I come after the saddle, unless I call him out."

He was for returning to the house, but just then the children saw their grandfather and his other guests coming in their direction.

"Maxwell," said Mr. Collingsworth, "I 've heard a heap of loose talk about this wonderful dog of yours. I lay you I have two can outfoot him; Dennis has another, and Kilpatrick another. Where 've you hid him? I don't mind dark horses in politics; but I don't like dark dogs in fox chases."

"Then you 'll not like Hodo," remarked Joe Maxwell, "for he 's very dark, almost black. Come, Hodo."

The hound instantly came from the shed, and stood looking at his master, his head turned expectantly to one side. This gesture, as you may call it, was somewhat comical, but it was impressive, too. Hodo was large for a hound, but very compactly built. His breast bone and fore shoulders were very prominent, his chest was deep and full, his hams were almost abnormally developed, and his tail ran to a keen point. His color was glossy black, except for a dash of brown and white on his breast and legs, and a white strip between his eyes. His ears were shorter than those of the average pointer. His shape and build were on the order of a finely bred bull terrier, only on a very much larger scale.

"You call that a hound?" remarked Mr. Collingsworth jokingly.

"If the Birdsong dogs are hounds," responded Joe Maxwell.

"He's a pretty dog," said Mr. Kilpatrick, "but he'll have some warm work cut out for him in the morning."

During this brief conversation Buster John had approached close to Hodo, and now laid his hand on the dog caressingly. Hodo flinched as if he had been stung, and snarled savagely, but instinct or curiosity caused him to nose the youngster, and then he whined and wagged his tail joyously, as if he had found an old friend.

"Well, well!" exclaimed Maxwell; "this is the first time I have ever known him to make friends with a stranger. He has two faults, a bad temper and a hard head."

HODO FAWNED ON BUSTER JOHN

Hodo fawned on Buster John and whined wistfully. Once he curved his tail in a peculiar fashion, and ran around, and hither and yonder, as if he were keen for a frolic. Maxwell was so astonished at these manifestations that he could do nothing but laugh. Hodo's antics, however, had attracted attention in another quarter. A brindle cur belonging to one of the negroes took offense at the playful spirit of the strange dog, and came rushing toward him, barking ferociously. The cur was as large as Hodo, and quite as formidable looking. The hound heard the challenge and rushed to accept it, and the two dogs came together some distance from the spectators. There was a fierce wrangle for the advantage, and then those who were watching the contest saw Hodo dragging the cur about by the neck and shaking him furiously. When Hodo finally gave him his liberty, the cur ran toward the negro quarters.

"I told you he was n't a hound!" exclaimed Mr. Collingsworth. "If he is, he 's not a common hound."

"I agree with you there," said Joe Maxwell, laughing.

Returning from his encounter, Hodo went to Buster John and rubbed his head against the youngster, and followed him about. This, of course, was very pleasing to Joe Maxwell; for ordinarily Hodo was very vicious with strangers, and especially with children.

When supper, which was a very substantial meal, had been discussed, Joe Maxwell called for Buster John and the two went to the lot. On the way there they were joined by Johnny Bapter.

"Show me where my horse is, Johnny Bapter," said Joe Maxwell.

"He right yonder, suh, in de best stall dey is. His legs all clean."

"Well, Johnny Bapter, I want fifteen ears of corn, not the biggest, with sound ends, and two bundles of fodder. Put the corn in the trough, untie the bundles of fodder outside, and whip as much of the dust out of it as you can. And then place a bucket of water in one end of the trough."

This was all very quickly and deftly done, for Joe Maxwell's tobacco, as Johnny Bapter described it, "tasted like mo'," and the way to get more was to look after that sorrel horse.

"I hope you are going along with us in the

morning," said Joe Maxwell to Buster John, as they were returning to the house.

"Oh, I wish I could!" the boy exclaimed; "I 'd give anything to go, but mamma says I 'm too young. She 's afraid something will happen to me."

Young Maxwell laughed. "Why, I went fox-hunting before I was as old as you. Mr. Dennis took me behind him twice, because I promised I would n't hunt rabbits with his fox hounds."

"Please tell mamma that!" cried Buster John.

"I certainly will," said Maxwell.

And he did. As soon as they went in the house, he took Buster John by the hand and went into the parlor where the lady was entertaining her guests with music and conversation. She was in high good humor. Her eyes sparkled and her laughter was pleasing to the ear.

"Come in, you two boys," she cried merrily. "Here 's a comfortable chair by me — shall I call you Mr. Maxwell? I used to call you Joe when you were younger."

"Everybody calls me Joe," said Maxwell. "I have come to ask you a favor. Will you allow Buster John to go hunting with us to-morrow morning?"

"Why, who ever heard of such a thing!"

"Mr. Dennis, there, has heard of it — twice."

The lady looked at Mr. Dennis, who gave an affirmative nod. "How would he go?" she asked.

"On my horse, behind me."

"What do you think of it, father?"

"Why, I think he will be perfectly safe with Joe."

"Let him go, by all means," said Mr. Dennis emphatically. "It will help to make a man of him."

"But two on a horse in a fox chase! Why, it's ridiculous," exclaimed the lady. "The horse would break down in half an hour."

"How much does Buster John weigh?" Joe Maxwell asked.

"Fifty-five," said Buster John proudly.

"Then the horse would carry a hundred and forty pounds. Mr. Dennis weighs at least thirty pounds more than that, and he's the smallest man in the party."

There was nothing for the mother to do but give her consent, though she gave it with many misgivings, as mothers will, and with many admonitions to Joe Maxwell to take care of the boy, which he faithfully promised to do.

To make sure that he would not be left behind, Buster John begged to be allowed to sleep in the room with Maxwell. This point was easily carried, and the youngster went off to bed triumphantly, an hour earlier than usual. He was asleep when the hounds were fed on warm corn-bread, especially prepared for them; and he was far in the land of dreams when, a little later, Joe Maxwell carried Hodo his supper, which Jemimy (bribed with tobacco for her pipe) had "saved out" for him. It was not large in amount, but carefully selected, and no doubt Hodo enjoyed it, for he made no complaint about it.

Buster John, as has been said, went to bed happy and triumphant, and it seemed to him that he had been in bed but a few moments when he felt Joe Maxwell shaking and rolling him about and heard him crying out: —

"Where 's this famous fox-hunter who was to go along and take care of me this morning? The horses are all ready, breakfast is ready (so Jemimy says), and everybody is ready except the Great North American Fox-Hunter, known far and wide as Buster John. What can be the matter with him?"

In this way Buster John was aroused to the realities, and he remembered with a thrill of delight that this was to be the day of days, so far as he was concerned. He leaped from the bed and was dressed in a jiffy.

"Don't wake the house, my son," said Joe Maxwell solemnly. "There's your overcoat your mother sent up last night; the air is chilly this morning. There was a cold rain during the night."

"But you have no overcoat," remarked Buster John.

"Oh, I'm tough," replied Joe Maxwell. "I've been out to look after my horse and dog. They are both prime, and the weather is prime. If the fox we are going after is a friend of yours, you may as well bid him good-by this morning."

"He's very cunning," explained Buster John. "A great many dogs have chased him. He is called Scar-Face."

"I've heard of him many a time," replied Joe Maxwell. "That's the reason I'm here to-day. If he's in the neighborhood this morning, and you get a good chance, tell him good-by."

"I think he knows all about this hunt," Buster John ventured to say.

"Oh, does he? Well, it will be a mighty good thing for him if he has moved his quarters; but we 'll beat around and about, and see if he won't give us a dare."

"I know where he used to stay," said Buster John. He did n't know whether he was doing right or wrong. "Aaron showed me."

"Aaron? Well, Aaron knows all about it, and he knows a good deal more than that. Some of these days I 'm going to write a book about Aaron."

"Sure enough!" cried Buster John. "I can tell you lots of things to put in it. I can tell you things that nobody would believe if they had n't seen 'em."

"Well, I 'll tell you what we 'll do," said Joe Maxwell. "We 'll make a bargain: you shall tail the fox to-day if you 'll tell me all about Aaron."

Buster John agreed, and the two shook hands over the contract in the most solemn fashion. In a few moments they were eating breakfast, which was a very good one for that part of the country, even if the coffee was made of parched rye and sweetened with honey. Shortly afterwards the hunters were ready to ride to the field. It was still dark, but dawn was beginning to show itself, and by the time the final start was made — the children's grandfather having to give some directions to Aaron — dawn was fairly upon them, and the chickens were fluttering from their roosts to the ground, and walking dubiously about in the half-light.

Now, old Scar-Face, confident of his powers, had done a very foolish thing. During the night, and while the rain was still falling, he had ventured to reconnoitre the Abercrombie place. He came out of the sedge-field through the bars, crossed the road, and went sneaking as far as the gin-house. Here he stopped and listened. The night was still, but his quick ears heard noises that would have been imperceptible to human ears — the playful squeak of a rat somewhere in the gin-house, a field mouse skipping through the weeds, the fluttering wings of some night bird. He heard the barking of dogs, too, but not a strange voice among them. He heard the Spivey catch-dog, with his gruff and threatening bark. Far away he heard a hound howling mournfully. The hound was evidently tied. Close at hand barked the cur that had challenged Hodo; he had not yet recovered his good humor.

But not a strange voice came to his ears. This was easily accounted for. The hounds that were to pursue him had been comfortably fed, and were now fast asleep, while Hodo was curled up in the shavings, dreaming that he had his mouth right on a fleeing fox, but could n't seize him. He whined and moved his limbs as he dreamed, and a prowling cat, that had paused to investigate the noise in the shavings, flitted away. All the sounds that came to old Scar-Face's ears were familiar; so from the gin-house he sneaked to the barn, as noiselessly as a ghost, pausing on the way to listen. Hearing nothing, he went further until he was under the eaves of the barn, in one end of which the horses of the huntsmen were stabled. Here he stopped and listened for some time. What could the silence mean? Peeping from the sedge-field during the afternoon, he had seen more than one horse and rider pass along the road, and several whiffs of strange dogs came to his sensitive nose. He concluded that these men and dogs meant another chase after him; but he was not certain, and so came forth in the dark to investigate.

Usually when hounds are taken away from home and fastened up out of sight of their masters, some of the younger ones will get lonely and begin to bark and howl. Old Scar-Face knew this well, but he did n't know that seasoned dogs rarely ever make such a demonstration unless they are hungry. Consequently, when he heard no barking and howling, he was almost convinced that, after a night's foray, he could return to the sedge-field and sleep undisturbed the next day. Still there was a doubt, and to ease his fears he decided to test the matter more fully.

On a fence near him a hen and half a dozen pullets were peacefully roosting. He crept up directly under the hen, gathered his strong legs under him, leaped upwards, and the next moment was cantering through the dry weeds dragging the squalling hen by the wing. Surely the racket was sufficient to alarm the plantation. At the barn he dropped the hen, placed a forefoot firmly upon her, and held his head high to listen. There was certainly a loud response to the hen's

PEEPING FROM THE SEDGE-FIELD

alarm. The geese in the spring-lot made a tremendous outcry, seconded by the guineas, but the only dog that barked was the cur that made the mistake of attacking Hodo.

This certainly seemed to be a fair test, and old Scar-Face was satisfied. He crushed the poor hen's neck in his cruel jaws, and put an end to her appeal for help. He was not very hungry, but he carried the hen home, promising himself a hearty breakfast in the morning. He ate a good ration, however, and then curled himself snugly together until he looked like a big ball of yellow fur.

He was awake early the next morning, but before he was half through his breakfast the light of day was beginning to creep under the briars; then he heard a long, mournful wail at the Abercrombie place, followed by another. How often he had heard this wail! It was the cry of foxhounds. He stayed not to hear it repeated, but skipped out into the gray dawn, like the shadow of Fear stealing away from the light.

X.

HODO GETS HIS BLOOD UP.

OLD Scar-Face would have had quite a shivery feeling if he had known that the wailing cry he heard was the voice of Mr. Kilpatrick's Music, telling the rest of the hounds that she had discovered the drag of a fox. Although Joe Maxwell, with Buster John behind him, and Hodo trotting in a dignified way at his horse's heels, had gone directly into the public road by way of the gate near the spring, the rest of the huntsmen, led by the White-Haired Master, went through the gin-house lot. The dogs, delighted to be free once more, and enthusiastic over the prospect of a chase, went galloping about the place, nosing in every corner; not because they expected to find the scent of a fox thereabouts, but because it is their nature.

It fell to the lot of Music to pass near the spot where old Scar-Face had caught the hen the night before. A few feathers were lying scattered about. These Music investigated, and immediately her nose made an important discovery. A fox had passed that way! Whereupon she lifted up her voice to warn the whole pack. Some responded, while others thought it was a piece of folly, and went trotting along about their business. But Music persisted.

Mr. Collingsworth stopped his horse and listened. "That 's a fox as sure as the world," said he.

"Pooh!" cried Mr. Dennis contemptuously; "you 've been training your dogs with a cat skin. Call the silly creature off, or you will have the whole pack going at full cry after a neighborhood tomcat."

Just then Mr. Dennis's Ruth put in: "What did I tell you?" he insisted. "If there 's a fox within a radius of five miles, this chase of a tomcat will scare him out of the country."

"Wait!" said Mr. Kirkpatrick. "I hear Whalebone trying to whimper, and I know mighty well he 's not interested in cats."

The rain had taken a good deal of the snap out of the drag, as Joe Maxwell explained to

Buster John afterward, but the hounds knew their business. They flung themselves about trying to hit upon a fresher scent, but finally worked back to the gin-house, from the gin-house to the road, and along the road to the bars. They worked very quietly. Music's warning wail had not been repeated, but she, as well as the rest, knuckled down to business, working with occasional whines and half-barks.

Joe Maxwell and Buster John had already arrived at the bars that opened into the sedge-field. When Hodo saw that all the rest of the hounds were coming in his direction, he lost his dignity so far as to examine the ground near the bars.

"If that fox was fool enough to go down to the barn during the night, he 's fool enough to stay in this field until he heard Music bark a while ago. If that 's so, he 'll never run ahead of the dogs any more." This was Joe Maxwell's conclusion.

Old Fountain, somewhat belated (for his going had not been decided on till the last moment), came galloping up, riding a mule, dismounted, and flung down the bars. Somehow, it seemed to Buster John that flinging down the bars had

JOE MAXWELL, WITH BUSTER JOHN . . . AND HODO

brought daylight; for, as the last one fell, he looked about him, and everything was plainly visible. He could see the rest of the hunters coming along the lane that led from the gin-house lot, and he could see Hodo cantering rapidly toward the pine thicket, where old Scar-Face had come at Aaron's call.

"When he 's up, where does he run?" Joe Maxwell asked Fountain.

"Straight to'rds de p'int er woods 'cross yander, an' den he b'ars ter de lef'—allers ter de lef."

At this instant Hodo gave a fierce challenge, to which Joe Maxwell responded with a cheerful halloo that brought all the dogs into the field with their heads up. The clouds had now blown away from the east, and the level beams of the rising sun fell upon the tops of the pines.

"Name er de Lord! Look at dat dog!" exclaimed old Fountain. Hodo had issued from the clump of pines and was now leaping in the air above the level of the sedge and running wildly about. The rest of the dogs were even more excited. They ran around, giving tongue and acting as if the fox was right under their noses. But Hodo suddenly ceased his antics, challenged twice, and was away, followed by the whole pack, their voices rhyming and chiming in the crisp morning air. Involuntarily Buster John squeezed Joe Maxwell as hard as he could. He was deliriously happy.

He felt a pang, however, when he saw the rest of the hunters galloping helter-skelter after the dogs, while he and Joe Maxwell were ambling along in a direction that seemed gradually to lead away from them. Butterfly, however, was running toward a hill in which the sedge-field culminated, and from this point a wide expanse of country lay under the eye.

Joe Maxwell looked at his watch, and found that only five minutes had passed since Hodo had led the hunt away from the clump of pines near which old Scar-Face made his home. The young man gave Butterfly his head, and in a few moments had reached the top of the hill, which, though not high, was the highest point for many miles. The sun, shining at their backs, threw a flood of yellow light on their hunt. Buster John could see his grandfather, tall and straight, riding after the hounds, flanked on either side by the rest of the huntsmen, while old Fountain brought up the rear, belaboring his mount with a brush broken from some convenient tree.

The dogs could be heard, but they were not in sight. They were running through the point of woods to which old Fountain had referred. While Buster John was looking at the hunters, Joe Maxwell ran his eye along the horizon to the left and caught sight of the fox going as swiftly as the shadow of a flying bird. He tried to show this swiftly moving shadow to Buster John, and finally succeeded; and then it vanished.

"Great goodness!" exclaimed Maxwell gleefully; "he must have stopped to catch a rat. What is he thinking about? He won't last forty minutes."

"Why, he's a mile or more ahead of the dogs," said Buster John.

"A mile and a quarter," admitted Maxwell, measuring the distance with his eye. "Wait till I send word to Hodo."

Prompt as an echo a black shadow hurled itself from the woods, and went careering across the open country. Joe Maxwell raised himself in his stirrups, placed both hands to his mouth, and uttered three short, sharp, shrill yells that cut through the air like a whiplash. Hodo answered with a roar, and seemed to grow smaller. Certainly he increased his speed. The rest of the dogs, headed by Whalebone, Ruth, and Music, were by this time well out of the woods, and the hunters, who were not far away, cheered them on. They were running beautifully, and Joe Maxwell could afford to say so.

"They 'll not be far away when the end comes," he remarked. "And if that old fox has any grit in him, he 'll be caught somewhere between this hill and the point of woods the dogs came out of."

"Why, he 's running away from here," cried Buster John.

"Of course," said Joe Maxwell, "and before many minutes have passed, he 'll discover that he can't play the old game. But if this is n't the old fox we 're after, we 'll never see the dogs catch him. They 'll be coming back presently, and we 'll have to see if there 's any hair between their teeth. If it is the old fox, he 'll run away till he hears Hodo close at hand, and then he 'll get scared and try to reach home again."

"The rest are following the dogs," said Buster John ruefully, as he saw them galloping in the sunlight.

"And you are sorry you're not with 'em?" suggested Joe Maxwell. "Well, they'll see no more of the race than we have seen, even if we're after the wrong fox. If we are after the right one, we'll probably have him ready for their inspection by the time they get back. But we're not going to stand here," he said reassuringly. "We are going to gallop over there and be ready to put Hodo right at his heels when he comes back."

This they did. In fact, Butterfly was chafing at the bit. Joe Maxwell let him have his head on the firm Bermuda turf, and he went flying along in a way that thrilled Buster John. A mile of this sort of traveling was enough to satisfy Butterfly's ambition for a while, and he was willing to stand quietly when his rider finally drew rein. The dogs could be heard running far away, their voices borne back on the morning breeze like the echoes of melodious complainings. Joe Maxwell looked at his watch again. The hunt had been going on twenty minutes.

"That 's the right fox," said the young fellow, "and he 's pretty game, or he would have made his double before this."

Finally the dogs went out of hearing altogether, and Buster John took advantage of that fact to follow with his finger on Maxwell's leg the entire outline of the triple loop by means of which old Scar-Face had been in the habit of throwing his pursuers off.

"If he had had an hour's start," said Maxwell, "this would have been a pretty performance, but he 's had his work cut out for him this morning. Maybe he was making one of his loops beyond the point of woods yonder. Yes, sir! That 's just what he was up to! The dogs came out of the woods not twenty-five yards from where they went in."

"Suppose the dogs have caught him?" suggested Buster John, who was all for action.

"No; they 're coming back," replied Maxwell.

"I don't hear them," said Buster John.

"Nor I," Maxwell admitted; "but Butterfly does."

And sure enough the thin and sensitive ears of

the horse pointed forward, and he was listening intently. Presently a murmuring, singing sound was heard, like the humming of bees. It grew louder by degrees, and seemed to be coming nearer and nearer.

"He 's due here pretty soon, if he 's on schedule time," said Joe Maxwell, in a low voice. "Keep perfectly still. Don't move. I want you to see how Hodo manages this sort of thing."

As the dogs topped a distant hill, their voices sounded like a clash of cymbals, with full brass band accompaniment. They seemed to be nearer than they really were.

"Yonder he comes," said Buster John, under his breath. He had his hand on Joe Maxwell's arm, and he indicated the position of old Scar-Face with his thumb.

The old fox was running bravely. He showed none of the usual symptoms of defeat or even fatigue. His brush was well up, and he was going very nimbly and rapidly. He soon disappeared, and the music of the pack died away as the dogs descended into the depression below the hill. Then came the sharp, eager cry of Hodo, close at hand. The watchers saw him come over a fence one hundred yards away, like a bird, and he ran toward them with head up and tail down. Evidently his blood was up.

He swept by some distance from the point where the fox had passed, and Buster John declared that he was not on the track at all. Joe Maxwell made no reply, but gave to Hodo the signal which told the dog that the fox was not far away. Again, as before, the dog increased his speed, bearing closer to the drag, and this time Joe Maxwell, with Buster John behind him, rode rapidly in a parallel direction.

"I give him five more minutes," said Hodo's master; "but he 's certainly a game old fox."

Faster and faster went Butterfly for several hundred yards, and then suddenly drew rein. The valley before them afforded a plain view, except for a ditch which ran through the middle. The dampness there had attracted a growth of alders, brambles, and such weeds and shrubbery as thrive where the ground is wet. On either side of this ditch there was a clear space of Bermuda turf, dotted here and there with small pine bushes. On the further side of this ditch Hodo was running. Suddenly he turned, crossed the ditch, and came flying back, while Joe Maxwell rode toward him as fast as Butterfly could go. Again Hodo crossed the ditch, and as he did so old Scar-Face came out on the opposite side and went careering across the open field. In a series of wild yells Joe Maxwell gave Hodo the view halloo, and in another moment the dog flung himself across the ditch again, and had old Scar-Face in plain view.

It is safe to say that never in the course of his life will Buster John ever experience such sensations as he then had, or behold such another spectacle as was there enacted before his eyes. He could only vaguely remember that he heard the cry of dogs behind him, and that the voice of Hodo sounded like a deep and continuous murmur. Within the course of fifty yards the dog overran the fox and turned and caught him before old Scar-Face could get himself under way.

And the funny part of it was that all the other dogs were up in time to give the dead fox a good shaking before he got cold.

When the hunters came up, Mr. Collingsworth pretended to believe that Rocket had killed the fox, and Buster John was astonished to see that

Joe Maxwell claimed nothing for Hodo. Mr. Dennis insisted that Rowan or Ruth was the guilty party, while Mr. Kilpatrick declared that if killing foxes was a hanging crime, he would n't give a thrip for Whalebone's life. These remarks were all jokes, some of them as old as the men that made them. But Buster John did n't know that.

"Why, the other dogs were not in sight when Hodo and the fox came into the field, and they did n't come up till the fox was caught and killed," Buster John asserted.

This statement seemed to make no impression on the others. "Abercrombie, make the boy tell you to-night how much Maxwell gave him to talk that way," remarked Mr. Collingsworth.

Seeing that Buster John's feelings were hurt, Joe Maxwell turned to him laughing. "They 're only joking," he explained. "They know very well that their dogs could never have caught this fox."

"Why, Hodo was running him all around here like a rabbit before the rest of the dogs were in sight, and before they did get in sight he had killed him," exclaimed Buster John.

THE DOG . . . HAD OLD SCAR-FACE IN PLAIN VIEW

"I believe you," cried Mr. Collingsworth. "That dog of yours is a freak, Maxwell; there 'll never be another like him. We'll have dogs that can catch red foxes — this pack here can do it any day in the week; but we 'll never see another dog with the 'go' in him that your dog 's got. Why, he 's venomous. Back yonder he crashed through a briar patch just like he 'd been shot out of a cannon, and his nose — well, he does n't have to run on the drag at all, much less put his head to the ground. I never saw anything like it in my life. There ain't a fox in the world that can stand up before him fifty minutes. Look at him! The other dogs are tired out, and he 's walking around as fresh as a daisy. No, sir! we 'll never see his like again."

"What 's your opinion, Fountain?" asked the White-Haired Master.

Fountain shook his head and dismounted from his mule, under pretense of fixing a buckle or strap.

"Well, suh," he said with fervor, "I has seed dogs in my time; I has seed dem what dey said could run, an' I has seed dem what I b'lieved could run, but not befo' dis day has deze eyes seed a dog what could reely run. Onless, suh, 't wuz dem ar greyhoun's what b'long ter Mars Billy Ross. Dem dogs has got de body an' de legs, but dey ain't got de head an' de win' er dish yer Hodo. Give um a mile dash in open groun' an' maybe dey could git dar 'fo' dish yer dog, but when it come ter brush an' briar and cane-brake, dey would n't show up nowhar close ter dat dog dar. Yes — yes, suh! — ef you 'd 'a' seed what I seed, you 'd 'a' rubbed yo' eyes like I did."

"What did you see, Fountain?" inquired the White-Haired Master.

"Well, suh, a breff of win' will tell it, but a preacher would n't make you b'lieve it." Fountain threw his head back and placed the fore-finger of his right hand in the palm of his left. "When ol' Scour-Face made his turn fer ter come back, he made it like a mule shoe — a wide sweep at de top, but narrer, as you may say, at de heels. De top er de turn mought 'a' been a mile broad — you-all may know better 'bout dat dan me — but at de narrer part a man stan'in' in de middle could 'a' seed de dogs gwine, an' could 'a' seed um comin'. I know, bekaze I seed whar dey went down a gully, an' I wuz settin' on dish yer mule in sight er de gully when I hear dat ar dog fetchin' ol' Scour-Face back.

"De fox, suh, come by me not twenty yards off, an' by de time he make his disappearance I hear dat dog open up not a hunderd yards behin', an' he come by me, suh, des like a bird a-flyin'. I fetched a whoop or two — you know how I kin holler, suh — an' de dog tuck a seven-rail fence an' never tetched it; no, suh, he never tetched it. You 'll not b'lieve it, suh, an' I don't blame you; but I kin show you whar de dog riz, an' whar he lit. You won't skacely b'lieve de tale yo' eyes 'll tell you when you see it; but dar 's de signs, suh, printed, as you may say, in de groun'. I fully 'spected he 'd ketch de fox right den an' dar; but ol' Scour-Face wuz a terror, suh, when it come ter gittin' over groun'. But dat dog — you may look at 'im yo'se'f, suh; all de rest pantin' fit ter kill, an' layin' down, an' him paradin' roun' here, smellin' de bushes an' lookin' like he ain't been in no chase. I said den, when he flung hisse'f over de fence, 'I 'll look at you right close de fust chance I git, kaze dey ain't no mo' like you, an' never is ter be!"

In this matter Old Fountain's judgment was as good as the best. Hodo had no forbears to account for his phenomenal gifts of nose and head and speed, and he left no posterity to succeed. He stands alone among fox hounds, unique and incomparable.

XI.

CAWKY, THE CROW.

After the fox hunt, Buster John felt that he had recovered some lost ground, as the saying is. Up to that time he had been somewhat handicapped by the experiences of Sweetest Susan. You will remember that it was Sweetest Susan who discovered the Grandmother of the Dolls. This was a very important discovery, too, for it led to the acquaintance of little Mr. Thimblefinger, and to the queer adventures of the children in the country next door to the world. More than that, Sweetest Susan had been kidnapped by the crazy man. It was natural, therefore, that Buster John should feel "put out," as he expressed it, by these events. But his talk with Mr. Bobs had led him to the manufacture of the wonderful bubble, and now he had witnessed a real fox hunt, perhaps the most interesting one that ever occurred in all that part of the country.

He did n't put on any airs about it, as some boys would have done, but he took pains to relate every event to his sister and Drusilla, just as it occurred, as far as he could remember it; and he patiently answered every question they asked him. For a long time the story of the fox hunt was the only piece of oral literature the children had to discuss, but there was always something new to be said of Hodo, or the sorrel horse, or Joe Maxwell.

Sweetest Susan hardly knew whether to feel sorry for old Scar-Face or not. Sometimes she was inclined to regret his taking off, but when she remembered the scream of the poor little rabbit, she was willing to believe that the old fox had received his deserts.

As for Drusilla, she had not a spark of sympathy for old Scar-Face. "I 'm glad dey cotch 'im," she said. "De dogs done 'im des like he done de yuther creeturs. An' 'pon top er dat, he sot up dar an' grin an' brag 'bout how he gwine ter outdo um. I hear ol' folks say dat dem what do de mos' braggin' is de mos' no 'count. I 'm glad dey got 'im. He had plenty time ter go 'way; he des hung 'roun' here kaze he b'lieve dey ain't no dog kin outdo 'im."

This sort of talk led, of course, to Joe Maxwell and Hodo, and before Buster John knew it, he would be describing the famous chase over again. For a long time this was interesting, but after awhile the small audience grew tired of hearing it, and Buster John grew tired of telling it.

Christmas and New Year's came and went, and were followed by weather so cold and stormy that the youngsters had to stay in the house, and Johnny Bapter had as much as he could do to keep the big hickory logs piled high enough in the wide fireplace. A fire big enough, it seemed, to roast an ox would hardly keep the dining-room or the sitting-room warm. It rained and sleeted, and then snowed, and the snow stayed on the ground long enough to give the children an opportunity to enjoy themselves on some clumsy sleds that Johnny Bapter made for them.

But toward the last of March a heavy rainstorm came roaring and sweeping along, and after that spring came out of her hiding-place and brought warm sunshine and the flowers with her. In a little while the peach orchard, which had looked so bleak and cheerless a few week before, seemed to be covered with pink snow, and the mocking-birds flew about singing.

Johnny Bapter had one sign for spring weather which he said never failed. "You see dem peach blooms? Well, ol' Jack Frost kin come an' nip um, but when you see an' hear de mockin'-bird singin' while he flyin', you kin go on an' plant yo' corn an' cotton, kaze dey ain't gwine be no mo' fros' dat season."

It was while the peach orchard was in full blossom that the children's mother chanced to remember that she had another supply of clothing for little Billy Biscuit, the waif who had been left with Miss Elviry Bobs, "to be called for," as the saying is. Naturally enough the children were keen to go; Sweetest Susan, because she wanted to play with Billy Biscuit, who, she said, was the cutest thing in the world, and Buster John, because he wanted to have another talk with Mr. Bobs. He had an idea that Mr. Bobs could tell him something new or show him something queer every day in the week, and Sunday too. Buster John was still loyal to Aaron. More than that, Mr. Bobs was so different from the Son of Ben Ali in all respects that there was no danger that admiration for one would clash with admiration for the other. Aaron was Aaron, and there was nobody like him but himself. Likewise Mr. Bobs was Mr. Bobs, quaint and original.

As both the children had a motive for going, they besieged their mother singly and collectively until finally she was obliged to surrender and give her consent. If she had known about the wonderful bubble, it is probable that she would have refused; but, since their experience with Mr. Thimblefinger, the children had grown somewhat reticent about their adventures. They had dropped hints here and there about what they had seen, but these hints were laughed at as crude and clumsy inventions, or as wild and impossible fiction.

One day Buster John, walking with his mother through the lot, burst out laughing at something the Muscovy drake said to the big white gander. He laughed so long that his mother concluded that he had hysterics. She carried him back to the house, and proceeded to dose him with hot and bitter drinks. He made matters worse by telling her what the drake had said to the gander, for she was then sure he was "flighty" in the head, and so he had to go to bed, though the sun was shining a warm invitation. He never made a similar mistake, nor did Sweetest Susan, after this terrible warning.

Drusilla finally consented to make one of the party, but she was particular to lay down the conditions under which she would give the youngsters the pleasure of her company. She held up her left hand with the fingers wide apart, and as she named the conditions she would register them by pulling the fingers together with her right hand.

"You-all say you want me ter go dar whar dat ol' man live at? I tell you right now I ain't achin' ter go dar, kaze I don't like de way he look out'n de eye; he chug full er rank venom. But ef I does go, I ain't gwine ter follow atter you in no foolishness. I ain't gwine in no bubble," — here she pulled the little finger of her left hand, — "I ain't gwine in no Fimblethinger doin's," — the third finger was pulled down, — "an' I ain't gwine nowhere ner do nothin' dat folks don't do when dey got der sevm senses," — here the middle finger was pulled down to join the other two.

These were the terms of the contract to which Buster John and Sweetest Susan were compelled to give their assent before Drusilla would consent to go.

"All dat," exclaimed Drusilla, "don't hender you-all frum gwine whar you choosen ter go. Ef you wanter git in bubbles an' git flew'd away wid, go an' git in 'um. Ef you wanter jump in springs an' pon's an' dream youer some'rs else, go ahead an' do it. But don't ax me ter do it; kaze ef you does you 'll have a great tale to tell Miss Rachel, an' she 'll gi' mammy de wink, an' mammy 'll gi' me a frailin'; well, I 'll take de frailin'; I 'd ruther be beat ter death on top er de groun' dan ter git flew'd off wid in a bubble, er drownded in dat ar Fimblethinger country."

The children faithfully promised that, no matter what happened or what they did, they would n't ask Drusilla to join them, and they would n't complain about her to their mother. This seemed to lift a heavy load from Drusilla's mind. She breathed freely and became even cheerful.

The journey to Mr. Bobs's house was in all respects a repetition of the former one, Johnny Bapter driving the two-seated spring wagon and singing blithely; and when they arrived at their destination, Miss Elviry was standing at the door with a smile of welcome. Little Billy Biscuit had grown considerably. He had larger ideas, too. He was no longer a calf in a pen, but a saddle-horse tied to the fence, a chair turned on its side answering all the purposes of a fence in this case. The bridle was a length or two of basting thread, and though it seemed to be a frail substitute for a halter, it must have been strong, for it served to hold this restive horse, which was making tremendous efforts to gain its freedom, pawing the ground and kicking out its heels at a terrible rate.

The earnestness of little Billy Biscuit was comical to see, and Sweetest Susan thought it was the finest spectacle she had ever witnessed. She wanted to hug the child then and there; but Miss Elviry shook her head.

"'T would upset him for the rest of the day," she explained. "Ef you want to please him, just say, 'Whoa, there!' Ef you git on wi' him, you 've got to believe in his make-believe. You would n't believe it, honey, but that child ain't half as much trouble as a grown person. Why, when you want him to be still, all you 've got to do is to tie him with some sewin' thread an' say he 's a hoss. A hoss he 'll be tell you come an' onloose him!"

The children entered at once into the spirit of the affair. At a word Sweetest Susan and Buster John became horses, and Drusilla was a mule. The change was effected as suddenly as the genii in the Arabian Nights could have accomplished it. No waving of wands nor incantation was necessary.

This drama of the horses was all very well for a little while; but the older children, being used to more variety, soon grew tired of it, and it was not long before they succeeded in coaxing Little Billy Biscuit out of doors. Just as they went into the yard, Miss Elviry suddenly remembered that she had forgotten to feed the hen with the young chickens that had just been "taken off;" so she mixed some corn meal and water in a tin pan, and began to call the hens.

The call was answered from overhead in the most unexpected manner. A crow, cawing and croaking, began to circle around Miss Elviry's head, and presently lit in the pan of dough.

"Oh, get away from here!" Miss Elviry cried

impatiently; "you 're allers stickin' yourself where you ain't wanted."

She pushed the crow from the pan, but he flew back with many croaks, and not until Miss Elviry had given him a good share of dough did he cease his flutterings. She dropped a wad of the food on the ground, and this the crow proceeded to devour, talking to himself all the while. Miss Elviry went to another part of the yard, hunting for the young chickens, but the children stood still and watched the crow.

"Ain't I done tol' you dey wuz cunjer people?" whispered Drusilla. "Why, you can't git in a mile er no crow less'n you been rubbin' agin deze folks. Now min' what I tell you; dis crow sho is Satan; you may follow atter 'im ef you wanter, but I ain't gwineter budge out'n my tracks!"

Little Billy Biscuit, however, was on very good terms with the crow. He sat on the ground by the bird, and with a small twig touched him occasionally on the legs. The crow saw the movement every time; but invariably he would raise the leg that had been touched, stretch out the toes on the foot and examine them carefully, uttering a croaky grumble all the time.

"WHAT IS YOUR NAME?" ASKED BUSTER JOHN

The solemn way in which he went about this was very amusing to the children. Buster John laughed so loudly that the crow stopped and looked at him sidewise, speaking for the first time so the children could understand him.

"Cackity! What's all the fuss about?" Then he went on eating the dough.

"What is your name?" asked Buster John.

"Cawky-ikey-uk-ek-ik-ak!"

"Well, Cawky, where did you come from?"

"Anywhere around here, ik-ek."

Miss Elviry came up at this moment, and, without knowing it, interrupted the conversation.

"One year the crows built in that pine thicket down yan'. He must 'a' fell from the nest, for one day I found him stretched out on the ground more dead than alive. I fetched him home an' nursed him till he could take keer of hisself. He goes off an' comes back, an' he's tamer than arry chicken on the place. He pays for his keep, too, for he's our crow-trap. I'll tell you about it before you go."

"Kuk-akity; how quick she talks! What did she say?"

"That you are her crow-trap," said Sweetest Susan.

"Ak-trap, trap-ak!" chuckled Cawky. "What is a trap?"

"Something that catches things," explained Buster John.

"Ekek, ak-ak-ak!" laughed the crow without smiling. "I know! In the corn row! Cackity! It's funny! Said one old crow to another old crow, 'What makes people do us so? For, you know, since we were born, it's been our trade to pull up corn.' Cack-ak, corn!"

There was something very quaint about Cawky as he walked back and forth, chuckling, laughing, and apparently trying to "show off" before strangers. He did it all so solemnly that it became comical, and the children were so much amused that they laughed till the tears came in their eyes; that is, they all laughed except Drusilla, who firmly believed that the crow was a bird of evil.

Once Cawky paused in his promenade, seized a ring that Sweetest Susan wore, and tried to twist it off.

"You better not let dat creetur fool wid you!" Drusilla exclaimed. "I tell you he de ol' Scratch; he'll grab you an' fly away wid you. You mark what I tell you!"

"Ek-ek-ek!" laughed Cawky, whose attention was attracted to Drusilla. "You have crows in your family! Cackity! I 'd like to catch that one in my trap."

"Huh! ef you wuz a crow, an' not de ol' Boy hisse'f, I 'd wring yo' neck," said Drusilla.

"Ek-nack, neck-ek!" chuckled Cawky, as he promenaded about, picking up flakes of mica, or glistening pebbles, or broken pieces of crockery.

At this point Miss Elviry returned and explained that in the spring, when the young corn was just sprouting and showing a tiny green blade above the soil, the crows did a good deal of damage. They would leave one of their number watching in the top of one of the tall pines, and the rest would fly down into the cornfield and pull up the young corn, row by row, to get at the grains still clinging to the tender roots. No one could approach near enough to shoot them, for the sentinel in the pine top would sound the alarm the moment a human being appeared in sight, and away all the crows would fly, to return promptly when the coast was clear.

One day, however, Miss Elviry heard a great clamor of crows in the cornfield, such a hubbub, indeed, that it attracted her attention. She went into the field; and there she saw the crows fluttering and flying about like mad. At first she thought they had attacked an owl or a hawk, but as she went nearer they all flew away but two. One of these was making tremendous efforts to fly, but the other, lying on his back, was holding him.

"'What in the world!' says I to myself," remarked Miss Elviry. "I went to where they was at, and there saw Cawky holding the other crow by the feet. The toes of the two was so tangled that 't was as much as I could do to ontangle 'em. That put the idea in my head that maybe Cawky would make a good crow-trap. So brother fixed up a couple of straps wi' pegs at the ends, an' we took Cawky out in the field, laid him on his back in a corn row, put the straps acrost his body, and pushed the pegs in the ground to hold him. Of all the squallin' an' jabberin' you 've ever heard! Cawky made more fuss in one minnit than a flock of crows make in a week. The crows fairly swarmed down on him in a little or no time, an' I run back for fear they 'd kill him; but he wa'n't hurt, an' he had another crow! Along at first,

Cawky did n't like it, but he 's got so now that when he hears crows about he 'll come a-flyin' and a-runnin', an' make the biggest kind of a fuss tell we git out his harness — we call it his harness — an' fasten him down in the field. I reckon they 've got some sign of distress like the Free Masons, for just as soon as he starts up his hollerin', all the crows in the settlement 'll come flyin' an' try to git him loose."

Again Miss Elviry went to attend to her household duties, leaving the children with Cawky, who, while she was talking, had been trying to pull the brass buttons from Buster John's jacket. He succeeded in getting one, and with this in his beak he ran around and around with his wings half-spread, and uttering loud cries of triumph. Then he ran under the house and hid it. He found the old house cat under there watching a mouse hole, and he ran her out and pursued her about until Miss Elviry had to take the broom to him.

It was great fun for the children, and Cawky seemed to enjoy it, too. But he subsided when Miss Elviry brought out the broom, and went stalking back to the children as solemnly as an old-time preacher.

"Why do you like to catch your cousins?" asked Buster John.

"Cackity! Because-ek they are my cousins, ek-ek!"

"Maybe you've already caught some of your brothers and sisters," said Sweetest Susan, using what Buster John called her Sunday-school voice.

"Ek! I hope so! I want-ek to catch my daddy and my mammy. Cackity! Did n't they push me from the nest and leave me on the ground in the rain and cold? Ek! I remember! And when I went back among them, did n't they drive me away? Cackity! They said I smelt like man. I've paid them well, and I'll pay them better. Ek-ek-ek!"

In the distance Buster John saw a chicken hawk circling around.

"Get under the house, Cawky; yonder comes a hawk."

"Ek-cackity! A hawk!" He rose in the air and flew to the top of a neighboring pine, and sat there swinging. The hawk came nearer and nearer, circling on motionless pinions, a picture of wild beauty.

CAWKY CATCHING CROWS

Suddenly Cawky rose in the air, and began to circle, too.

"Kerray-kerree!" This was the war-cry of Cawky's brethren. Twice or thrice repeated at intervals, it meant a hawk. Repeated a dozen times with no interval, it meant that an owl had been discovered asleep in the woods.

The hawk made a lusty effort to escape, and would have succeeded if Cawky had been without allies, but in every direction crows were seen rising in the air — some ahead of the hawk, some behind her, and some on each side. Rising and circling, she suddenly swooped and struck at Cawky, but missed him by a hair's breadth, as she came down with a rush and a swish. It was a fierce, but foolish move. Before the hawk could recover herself, the whole colony of crows was upon her, and then began a battle royal, which could have but one result.

The hawk was fierce and desperate, her talons were sharp and her beak was strong. The crows had no talons, but their beaks were numerous. More than one was compelled to fly heavily away as the result of a moment's contact with the hawk, but finally the boldest among them found a place on the hawk's back, out of reach of beak and talons, and bore her slowly to earth, where, in the course of a few moments, she was killed outright.

The children ran forward as hard as they could when they saw the hawk falling, but she was dead when they reached the scene, and Cawky was strutting around her, chuckling and talking to himself, ready to strike her with his strong beak if she showed any sign of life.

There was nothing to do but to carry the hawk to the house as a trophy, and show her to Miss Elviry, who expressed great satisfaction, and gave it as her firm and unalterable opinion that it was the very same hawk that had been snatching her young chickens right from under her nose for two seasons past. No doubt Miss Elviry was right, for the hawk was very large and fat.

By that time Johnny Bapter had returned from his errand to Harmony Grove. He called the children and they clambered into the wagon, and by dinner time they were safe at home.

XII.

THE STORY OF MR. COON.

AARON smiled when the children told him how Mr. Bobs could set a crow to catch a crow. He said the same plan had been practiced for many long years. He had heard his father, Ben Ali, tell about it. Indeed, the probability is that out of this practice the saying, "Set a thief to catch a thief," had arisen, for nobody could trust a thief to catch a thief unless the first thief was securely fastened.

But Aaron, on his side, had something quite as interesting to tell the children. From a negro whom he knew he had secured a raccoon,— a genuine, full-grown raccoon. This was news, indeed, and so exciting in its character that Aaron was compelled to answer, or to parry, volley after volley of questions.

"Oh, how old is it? and what does it look like?" cried Sweetest Susan.

"And who is it to belong to? and is it tame, — so tame that you can put your hand on it?" asked Buster John.

"Why did n't dey kill it an' cook it?" inquired Drusilla.

Aaron put his fingers in his ears. He could n't answer all the questions put to him. Finally there was a lull in the excitement.

"What did you give for him?" Buster John asked after a pause.

"Something," replied Aaron smiling.

"But how much?"

"Enough."

"Shucks," cried Buster John; "if I had known there was some great secret about it, I would n't have asked."

Aaron pinched the boy's ears gently, and said, "Come!" He went to his cabin, the children following, and when they went in, the first thing they saw was Mr. Coon, pacing back and forth the length of the small, steel chain which held him. He paused and regarded them curiously, twisting the end of his sharp nose about, and mechanically feeling in the cracks of the floor with his forepaws, which seemed to be as supple and as useful as a boy's hands.

When Buster John went nearer, Mr. Coon raised himself on his hind legs and uttered a cry almost identical with the scream of a rooster when a bird suddenly flies over, or a hawk appears in sight. Buster John knew it was a warning, and so he stopped.

"What is the trouble, Frog-Eater — Tadpole-Catcher?" the Son of Ben Ali sharply inquired.

"You can't fool me," snarled Mr. Coon. "I 've seen creatures like him before. They poked my sides with sticks, and pulled my tail."

"But this one is different, Bug-Eater," said Aaron.

"Oh, call me what you please, Son of Ben Ali. I was glad to come with you, but I did n't invite myself here, did I? If you were hungry and thirsty and tied fast, and saw coming toward you one of the creatures that had made misery for you, would you grin and say, 'Welcome, friend'?"

"Likely not," replied Aaron. "But you have been fed, Frog-Eater. You said you had enough."

"Enough of the kind, Son of Ben Ali; yes, and too much. If you want me to eat corn, get some that is soft on the cob and juicy. If you want me to be nice, fetch me a couple of young chickens, or a handful of black beetles." Sweetest Susan shivered.

"Well, Tadpole-Catcher," said Aaron, "if you want good things to eat, go with these friends. They have been touched. They know everything you say, and when you are hungry or thirsty, you have only to give the sign."

At this Mr. Coon paced back and forth very rapidly. This was the way he showed his impatience. He was anxious to go with them. Aaron unfastened the chain and placed one end in Buster John's hand. The youngster held it very gingerly, and was inclined to shrink when Mr. Coon came too close, but he soon got over that feeling, and so did Sweetest Susan and Drusilla; so that, in a little while, they were more familiar with Mr. Coon than they had ever been with any of their pets.

They lost no time in giving him his dinner, which consisted of chicken heads and giblets. Mr. Coon smacked his mouth over them, and when he had finished declared that he felt better than he had for many a day, and remarked: —

"*Eg liblum gig loblum og iggle!*" which literally translated means "Big dinner, bigger bed." Freely interpreted, it means: "If I continue to get such fine fare, I'll have to get my clothes made larger."

It may interest readers who are no longer young to know that in the language of animals the root word lablam stands for things, and its variations, liblum, loblum, leblim, liblom, etc., mean the thing at hand, or, to be more exact, the thing under the nose — the thing talked about.

It is a pity that Joe Maxwell, who is responsible for these dry details, did not take the trouble to write the language down from Buster John's recipe. But he put it off from day to day, and now there is nothing left but the rough notes of these stories, and some scattered fragments of explanation, one of which is presented above.

Well (to shoo all this away) Mr. Coon was highly delighted with his dinner, and was ready to curl up and take a nap, or was willing to join the children in a frolic. So they led him into their playroom in the attic, unsnapped the chain from his collar, and gave him the freedom of the wide space.

First, Mr. Coon must poke his nose or his forepaws into everything. He paced round and round the room, smelling at or feeling in every nook and cranny. When he was satisfied with his inspection, nothing would do but he must feel in Buster John's pocket. He pulled out marbles, nails, and fragments of chinaware, which the youngster used in place of money. With a few fragments of fine chinaware in his pocket, Buster John always felt rich. With this form of currency he had bought whole droves of ponies and large arsenals of guns, pistols, swords, and war cannon from imaginary venders.

Piece by piece Mr. Coon brought Buster John's treasures to light, and examined them carefully. The children noticed that Mr. Coon's forepaws were very much like tiny hands, and that his hind feet made tracks in the sand that looked like those of a wee baby. Of course, it was Sweetest Susan who made this discovery. Whenever Mr. Coon left the prints of his feet visible, one could almost imagine that some small goblin in human shape had passed that way, going on all-fours. Almost! Why, Sweetest Susan did imagine it — was sure of it, indeed — whenever

MR. COON . . . EXAMINED THEM CAREFULLY

she was in Make-Believe land, where she lived most of the time. Surely it could not be more wonderful than the country next door to the world, where old Mr. Rabbit and Mrs. Meadows and the looking-glass children had their abode.

For a few days Mr. Coon feasted, and then the children thought he should begin to pay for his board; first, by giving an account of himself, and next in any other way that might be devised. So far as Mr. Coon was concerned, he was perfectly willing to accommodate the children. He was never bad tempered unless he saw a cat or dog, and such of these as were about the house and yard soon learned to give him a wide berth, for his claws and teeth were sharp, and he was a born fighter.

In Joe Maxwell's rough notes, Mr. Coon began thus: —

"If I had to tell my tale from the talk-thing, as you talk your talk, I 'd talk no talk of this thing." As this would be hard to follow, it has been rendered into a free translation from first to last.

"If I had to learn my language out of books, as you do yours," said Mr. Coon, leaning back in a corner of the playroom, and rubbing his face and nose with both hands, "I would n't have much to say about myself, for I would n't know how to say it. My home was in the hollow limb of a tree, and I can remember how nice it was to sleep in that soft, warm place. There were four others besides me, and we used to sleep close together till our mammy came home. We were always awake when she came, for we could hear her climbing the tree; and then, if it was not raining, she 'd sit on the outside, and dry her feet and clothes with her tongue. Sometimes we 'd get impatient and begin to cry, and once one of the others went to the door; the slap he got made him squeal, and none of us ever bothered our mammy any more by going to the door. But, my! How hungry and angry I used to get while mammy sat out there cleaning her feet and drying her clothes! But she always took her own time, and then, when she came in, what a scramble there was for the right teat. Mine was the middle one, but I always had to claw and be clawed before I could get it. We were all ravenous, and I never did get as much food as I wanted at one time till I came here. I think our kind are born hungry, and kept hungry that we may be able to escape from those that follow us.

"The first thing I really remember was once when I heard a bird chirping and whistling right at our very door. I trembled and shook all over. The others were asleep, and I was glad of it. Shaking and trembling, I crept to the door, and there, right at me, was a bird with a long bill, which he was poking under the bark. Shivering and shaking, I jumped on him, but I came near falling to the ground. He was stronger than he seemed to be, and he had claws, too. He clinched me with these, and beat me over the head with his wings, but I did n't mind that. I did n't mind anything. I shook no longer. I felt my hair rising on my back; I heard myself growl. I did n't know why, but I was furious. I crushed the bird in my teeth until his wings ceased to move; but I was still angry; I had tasted blood; I had made my first kill. If one of the others had come out just then, I think he would have been sorry. But they were all frightened by the noise and were huddled in the farthest corner. Then, when I was no longer angry, but proud, I went to the door carrying the bird in my teeth. They smelt the blood and rushed at me, and then there was a fight!"

"Why, you were fighting your own brothers and sisters!" said Sweetest Susan severely.

"So would you, if you were of my kind," replied Mr. Coon. "There was a fight, but they all got a piece of the bird. After that we were changed. It seemed as if we had been asleep all the time, and something had suddenly awakened us. Then mammy came home. She sniffed around and smelt the blood and saw the feathers. She nosed under us as we lay and rooted us out of the way, but she found nothin' more than feathers. 'Well, I declare!' she cried; 'who 's been bringing you a bird?'

"'Is that what you call a bird?' asked one of the others, and when she said it was, they all squalled out, 'Oh, mammy, mammy! Fetch us some more! Mammy, fetch us some more!'

"But she kept on asking, 'Who brought this one? Who brought this one?' I said nothing, but the others looked at me and said I was the one that brought the bird.

"'Where did you get it?' mammy asked.

"I told her I had grabbed the bird, and though she said nothing she seemed to be pleased, and I noticed that she combed my hair with her tongue a great deal longer than she ever did before. After that, she began to bring us birds and frogs, and once she brought us a big fish, and that was fine."

"Frogs!" cried Drusilla. "You hear dat? Frogs!"

"Not the kind that live on land," explained Mr. Coon, making a wry face, "but the kind that hide on the bank of the creek and jump in when they hear you coming. You have to take many long and hard lessons before you can catch one. Fish are easier to catch. You turn your back to the creek, let the tip of your tail touch the top of the water, and move it about — and wait."

"Huh! I see myself!" exclaimed Drusilla resentfully.

"Hush up," said Buster John; "you 're no coon."

"Well, some folks call niggers coons," replied Drusilla.

"All this time," Mr. Coon continued, paying no attention to the interruption, "you leave your body turned half around so you can see what is going on in the water. When the fish shows himself, you reach down and flirt him out on the bank, and in reaching you have to be quicker than the fish — and fish are mighty quick. But a gnawing stomach" (*dag ig lublum;* literally, *crying-for-meat-thing*) "makes a quick hand.

"Well, mammy was trying to teach us all these things, and we were learning very fast. She took us with her when the sun was low, or when it had just gone away, and, though the light was trying to our eyes, we did very well. Once mammy heard a dog barking, and she hurried us home, making us run as hard as we could. I asked her what the trouble was, and she said it was the barking of the dog that scared her; and she told us that when we were older and heard a dog bark we must hurry home by a roundabout way, and run in the water whenever we could, because dogs had a way of smelling where we went along and following us wherever we went; and if they followed us home they 'd sit at the foot of the tree and bark until a man would come with a sharp cut-thing and hit the tree until it fell.

"All these things we learned, and a great many more, but you know what fool things young things are."

"I ain't ol', but I know I ain't no fool," interrupted Drusilla.

"Oh, will you hush?" cried Buster John.

"You know what fool things young things are," repeated Mr. Coon. "They listen to what their elders say, and think it is nothing but talk. The young thing is always a smarter thing than the old thing, and sometimes he is too smart. I remember that one night I slipped away from the others after mammy had been gone a long time. I was careful to make no noise on the tree, but when I reached the ground, I felt so happy that I jumped in the air and whirled around for joy. The air was cool and fresh, the swamp smelt good, and the dark was fine. I could see everything ever so much better than when the big shine-thing is blazing over the trees.

"So I shook myself and started for the pond in the swamp. There I caught some small fish, and they tasted ever so much better than those mammy brought home. Then I wandered out of the swamp and went on the hill where the brambles are, hunting for birds and birds' nests. I found two birds and one nest with tiny eggs in it, and the eggs tasted so nice that I wanted more, and I went rambling all over the hill ever so far. Suddenly I heard a dog bark. The sound of it made me shake and shiver, and I stood listening. Presently I heard the bark again, and it was so close at hand that it sounded like a dreadful roaring."

"I boun' you had ter hump yo'se'f den," suggested Drusilla.

Mr. Coon, with his eyes half shut, for he was sleepy, kept right on the track of his narrative.

"A dreadful roaring. I went away from there as fast as my legs could carry me, and ran right to the swamp. I could hear the dog coming, too; and, far off, I could hear some one crying out."

"That was the man cheering the dog," Buster John explained.

"The dog," said Mr. Coon, "seemed to be coming closer and closer, and I began to run harder than ever. I remembered that my mammy had said something about water and dogs, and I ran straight for the big pond in the swamp; the

Son of Ben Ali knows where it is. I slipped into the water and swam to the middle, where there 's a stump of an old tree. I had hardly reached it when the dog came in sight on the bank of the pond, and began to whine and bark. He ran around to see if I had gone out on the opposite side, and then he caught sight of me. He jumped into the water with a great splash, and when I saw him coming, fear seemed to leave me. I climbed upon the stump, and when he came near I jumped on his head and bit him on the neck with all my might. He went under, but I turned him loose, and came to the top and swam around and round. He came up trying to shake the water from his ears, and they flapped on the pond like the wings of a duck that is trying to rise in a hurry. Before he got through flapping I had jumped on his head again, and when he went down I clawed him with my hind feet. He tried to cry out, but all he could do was to make bubbles on the water. I jumped on his head twice after this, and the third time he never came up any more. I went out on the bank, shook the water off my clothes, and cantered toward home. As I went along, feeling very proud,

I heard the man calling his dog. First he blew a horn. He blew it a long time, and then called and called; but the dog, being at the bottom of the big pond, could make no answer.

"When I reached home I found mammy there. She had heard the dog bark, and had made haste to get out of his way. Then, finding one of her children missing, she knew that something had happened or was going to happen. She was sure of it. She heard the dog running, and she knew the missing young one would be caught. If he was n't caught, she hoped he would be badly scared; it would serve him right for not obeying the rules she had made.

"When I got home, you may know I was tired. Mammy dried my clothes while I told her what had happened, and she would hardly believe it; but she could plainly hear the man calling his dog, first with his voice and then with his horn. He kept that up for some time, and finally, on his way home, he passed right under our house, calling his dog and tooting his horn; and I was the only one of the family that dared to look out as he went by.

"Well, I had no more adventures until one

night, having come home myself, I heard a crowd of dogs barking. The noise they made grew louder and louder, and presently I heard mammy climbing the tree as hard as she could. She came up so fast that I could hear pieces of bark fall to the ground. She was scared nearly to death.

"'They are after me,' she cried, 'and I did n't have time to take to water!' Sure enough, the dogs came charging through the bushes, howling and panting like mad, and they gathered around the tree and howled and barked until the men came up with torches. I was curious to see what was going on, though the others were too frightened to move. I came out and sat on the limb and looked down at them. They were all black men, except one. The one that had the biggest torch held it behind him and moved it back and forth behind him.

"'There he is,' he yelled, 'I see his eyes!' The man with a cut-thing began to hit the tree. I never knew what was going to happen until the tree began to sway. Then I could feel it falling. As it fell, I ran down the tree until I came to one of the largest limbs, and, by the time I had climbed that, the tree hit the ground with a noise that sounded as the clouds sound when they clap together and make a big, quick shine. The limb shook so hard that I came near falling off; but I held on the best I could, and in a moment I heard a great noise of fighting, screaming, howling, and growling. I was wild with fear, but I could do nothing. Close to the limb I was clinging to was a black man holding a torch. The light blinded my eyes, and the hot smoke stifled me. I thought none had seen me, but the man who was not a black man was standing apart from the others, and when I looked at him I found he was looking at me.

"I kept looking at him, and he at me, until I was no longer afraid. I had the feeling that he was a friend" (*close to cousin-thing*), "and I wanted to go to him. But how could I? It was the Son of Ben Ali, and he said nothing to the others. But the thick smoke came in my nose, and I sneezed. The black man yelled, 'Here 's another!' and climbed on the tree. He was about to strike me with the torch, but the Son of Ben Ali said, 'Wait!' He came to the limb, stretched out his hand to me, and I touched

"I WAS WILD WITH FEAR"

it with my tongue. 'Come,' he said. I jumped to his shoulder and felt safe; but when he carried me among the strange ones, when I saw the dogs nosing around with blood on their ears, and when I saw my mammy and the others lying there moving no more, fear came again, and but for the Son of Ben Ali's hand and voice I should have jumped down into the middle of the pack.

"The Son of Ben Ali gave me to a friend to take care of, and though I went hungry many a time, it was not the fault of the black man. Maybe he was hungry himself, and his wife and children, too; or maybe he was too busy to remember me. But now I'm here, and if you'll excuse me I'll take a nap."

Mr. Coon opened his mouth wide to gape, cuddled down in the corner, and was soon sound asleep.

XIII.

FLIT, THE FLYING SQUIRREL.

Mr. Coon was a nine days' wonder with the children, but it fell out with him as it falls out with everything we possess — he ceased to be interesting. He was not neglected so far as his food was concerned, but he ceased to be the centre of attraction. Other things won the attention of the youngsters, who were in no wise different in this respect from other children, or from their elders. Especially was this the case when, one day, Aunt Minervy Ann, who was going to move to town with her former master, came to bid them all good-by. To Aunt Minervy Ann this going to town was like traveling to some foreign country, though the town was but a short distance from her old home.

She came to say good-by to all the children, as well as to the grown folks. On her arm she had a small basket, and this, she declared, contained a small present for Buster John and Sweetest Susan.

"Ef you had ter guess what 't wuz 'fo' you got it, I 'd hafter tote dis basket back home widout takin' de led off." So much she said by way of preface.

"It 's a bird," Sweetest Susan guessed.

Aunt Minervy Ann laughed and shook her head. "It can fly some," she admitted; "but 't ain't no bird."

"It 's a bat," guessed Buster John.

"Dey ain't no feathers on it; but 't ain't no bat."

"Well, it can't be a flying fish," said Buster John.

Again Aunt Minervy Ann shook her head. "'T ain't no flyin' fish. Ef you want flyin' fish, you 'll hafter go ter dem what seed um fly."

"Why don't you guess, Drusilla?" said Sweetest Susan.

"Kaze I already know what 't is," replied Drusilla.

"What is it, den?" snapped Aunt Minervy Ann.

"It 's a whipperwill. Dat 's what 't is," replied Drusilla.

"Ef I had de will, I'd whip you here an' now!" exclaimed Aunt Minervy Ann earnestly; "dat's how much whipperwill I got in dish yer basket."

"Don't tell us what it is," said Buster John. "Just tell us a little something about it, and let us guess."

"Well," replied Aunt Minervy Ann, "it kin fly, yit 't ain't got no wings ter flop. It makes a nes' in de tree, and yit 't ain't no bird."

"Oh, I know what it is!" cried Sweetest Susan; "it's a — it's a — what is it, brother? You know."

"I'm glad you think so," said Buster John. "But if I was going to make a sure enough guess, I'd say it is a flying squirrel."

"Dar, now!" exclaimed Aunt Minervy Ann, laughing. "De mule's yone." This was a current expression among the negroes when they surrendered an argument or settled a contention. The one who was shown to be in the wrong in any matter would say, "De mule's yone."

So Aunt Minervy Ann carefully lifted the cover of the basket, reached her hand in, and drew forth the cunningest and most beautiful

"DEY AIN'T NO FEATHERS ON IT; BUT 'TAIN'T NO BAT"

little creature the children had ever seen — the daintiest and cutest of all the tribe of four-footed animals.

As might have been expected, Sweetest Susan went into ecstasies over this wonderful little creature, which can fly without wings; and which, though it is the wildest and most elusive of animals, is tame the moment it is captured. It lay cuddled in Aunt Minervy's hand in apparent content, and closed its pretty eyes as she gently stroked it.

"Oh, it's mine! it's mine!" cried Sweetest Susan.

"Well, take it then," said Buster John, with apparent generosity.

Sweetest Susan held out her hands, and then drew them back, as her brother knew she would. "Is it quite tame?" she asked.

"He's tame ter me," responded Aunt Minervy Ann. "I cotch him yistiddy."

"Then he's *not* tame," said Sweetest Susan decisively, putting her hands behind her.

She was sorry the next moment, for Buster John, remembering what he had heard old Fountain say about the harmlessness of flying squirrels, and how sinful it was to kill them, since the act always brought bad luck, lifted the little creature tenderly from Aunt Minervy Ann's hand and placed it in his own. Then, relenting a little, he placed it in Sweetest Susan's hand.

Aunt Minervy Ann nodded her head vigorously at this, and drew Buster John toward her, exclaiming, "Ef you allers do dat, you 'll make a fine man, — a mighty fine man!" And, strange as it may seem, though Buster John forgot most of the fine-spun advice received from his elders, he never failed to remember this simple statement of Aunt Minervy Ann's. Perhaps it was because Aunt Minervy Ann's words were charged with earnestness. Anyhow, they stuck in the lad's mind and stayed there.

It was all Sweetest Susan could do to keep from "loving the flying squirrel to death," as she said. Its coat was as smooth, and as soft, and as fine as silk, and it seemed to enjoy the stroking and gentle caresses to which Sweetest Susan subjected it. Even Drusilla was delighted with the flying squirrel, and wanted to hold it in her apron, being afraid to touch it with her hands.

"He 's mighty purty," she said; "but I tell

you now, he got long tushes in dem little jaws. Ef you don't b'lieve me, you kin des look an' see."

Buster John and Sweetest Susan were too much interested in the beauties of the little creature to expose any of its ugly features, even if it had any. They had never seen a flying squirrel before. There were many of this species on the place, but they were so shy and elusive that the children caught only fleeting glimpses of them between sunset and dark. They could see something flit before their eyes, swooping from some tall tree nearly to the ground, then circling upward to another tree; they could hear a chirping curiously like that of a sparrow, and the flying squirrel would be gone — if it could be said to have come. Therefore the little fellow in hand was twice precious, once for the sake of its beauty, and once for the sake of its rarity.

"I don't see how anybody ever cotch one un um," remarked Drusilla. "You see um — flip! — an' deyer gone!"

"How did you catch him, Aunt Minervy Ann?" asked Sweetest Susan.

"I ain't got time ter tell you right dis minnit,"

replied Aunt Minervy Ann. "I'll go tell de niggers on de place good-by, an' den I 'll come back, an' ef you ain't fin' out fer yo'se'f, I'll up an' tell you — kaze I hear a heap er talk 'mongst my color how A'on done larnt you-all how ter talk wid de creeturs. I ain't never b'lieved it myse'f; but if you-all tell me how I cotch 'im atter I come back fum de quarters, den I 'll know it 's so. Dey 's sump'n in me dat tells me right pine-blank dat ef folks can't talk wid de creeturs it 's der own fault; an' yit, when you come ter think 'bout it hard an' strong, it don't look natchual."

Aunt Minervy Ann went her way for the time being, and Sweetest Susan, holding the flying squirrel against her rosy face, said: —

"Your name is Flit. Remember that, please. Now, Flit, you must tell us something about yourself and how you happened to let Aunt Minervy Ann catch you."

"Who is that talking?" chirped the flying squirrel. "I 'm awfully sleepy. This is my time for sleeping. What is 'Flit'?"

"Flit is your name, I 'd have you to know," replied Sweetest Susan, "and I want you to tell us about yourself."

"Well, give me some water," said Flit (his words sounded like the notes of the song sparrow), "and don't keep me awake too long. I did n't have any sleep yesterday, and I have n't slept any to-day."

"You should be good and sleep at night," Sweetest Susan declared.

"I can't sleep when I'm hungry, and when the shine-ball goes down I have to wake and hunt for food. I'm awfully sleepy now, and hungry, too!"

"Whar dat box er scaly-barks you-all had?" inquired Drusilla. "Ef you'll git some, I'll go crack um."

"What are scaly-barks?" asked Flit.

"Small hickory nuts," replied Sweetest Susan.

Instantly Flit was wide awake, making a chattering noise such as a small bird might make. "That is the very thing I want. Make haste, make haste!" he cried.

Drusilla was soon cracking the scaly-barks, and in a few moments Flit was sitting on his hind legs in Sweetest Susan's hand, eating the "goody," as the children called it, as fast as Buster John could pick it out with an old shoemaker's awl. The little creature was very dainty about it, too. If the meat of the scaly-bark happened to be the least spoiled or worm-eaten, he promptly rejected it and called for better food. And between times he told of some of his recent adventures.

"Not so very long ago," said Flit, looking curiously at a piece of the meat of a scaly-bark, and turning it over and over in his nimble forepaws, "I went home before the shine-ball came out, and there I found a big black snake curled up in my bed. He raised his head and made his tongue quiver, and I was afraid to go in. I did n't know what to do. I knew if the shine-ball came out and found me away from home that I would n't be able to see what was going on, for the shine-ball is so bright that it hurts my eyes.

"I wandered about among the trees, jumping from one to the other, until finally I remembered where a woodpecker had had a nest in a big pine not far off. I had seen him hiding some acorns there, and at night I used to go there and see how they tasted, and I thought if I could get there by the time the shine-ball came out I could get a little rest. Well, I went to the pine and crawled into the woodpecker's nest. But it was very uncomfortable, and had a bad smell. There was no soft bed in it, such as I had at home, and everything about it was rough. The door — Now I don't think you ought to eat all the good ones yourself and pick out the bad ones for me. Why, that last piece was black on one side."

This was addressed to Buster John, whose appetite for scaly-barks had asserted itself when he began to pick out the "goodies" for Flit.

"There — now that 's better," said Flit, with a satisfied chirp. "The door of the woodpecker's house looked towards the place where the shine-ball comes from, and everything about it seemed to be wrong. But it was the best I could do. I crept in and curled up for such sleep as I could get in such a place. I went to sleep, too, for I was very tired. How long I slept I don't know, but when I woke I was hot. The shine-ball was looking right in the door, and I was nearly suffocated."

At this point Flit pretended to sneeze to show how he suffered from the heat.

"There was only one thing to do, and this I did. I crawled out and went halfway down the tree, where the trunk was large enough to hide the shine-ball. There I stretched myself out on a limb and tried to believe I felt better. Did I tell you the tree was dead? Well, it was. Outside of the woodpecker's home there was n't a hiding place in it. The pine was standing alone, and the only way to reach the thick woods where I lived was to travel a part of the way on a zigzag fence.

"Now, I don't like to do this. To be out in the light is bad enough, but to travel on a fence with a shine-ball and everything else looking at you is worse still. So I stretched out on the big limb not far from the ground, and tried to be content. I don't know how long I lay there, but all of a sudden I felt the wind rushing down on me, and under the limb I went like a flash — and none too soon, for as I went under, a big hawk came swishing by so close that I could almost feel her feathers brush me. Well, I was so frightened I began to pant. I had often heard of hawks, and had been warned against them, but I never saw one before. Did you ever see one? They are terrible.

"This hawk was not satisfied. She swooped

and circled as I do when I make a long flying jump from tree to tree. She circled upward and sailed around overhead. I could n't see very well for the glare of the shine-ball."

"What de name er goodness is de shine-ball?" inquired Drusilla.

"Why, it 's the sun, goosey," answered Sweetest Susan.

"I could n't see very well," said Flit, "and so I went on top of the limb again; but I had hardly stretched out there, thinking the hawk was gone, when I felt the wind again, and this time she did n't miss me more than the width of one of my whiskers. Up went the hawk again, and I thought it would be best for me to stay under the limb. But this did n't help me much. The hawk began to call her mate, and in a very short time there were two of them sailing around. The biggest one came slowly down and lit on the limb right over me. She leaned forward and looked at me; and of all the horrible creatures you ever saw, she was the most horrible. She breathed as loud as a 'possum snores.

"I came very near dropping from the limb. I moved toward the body of the tree, and the hawk moved after me and tried to reach me with her hooked beak. I made a dash and went round the body of the tree, and as I did so the hawk's mate came swooping down. By this time the other hawk was on the wing, and by the time I darted on the other side she was ready to swoop. This would n't have lasted long. Some one came along and said 'shoo' to the hawks, and they flew away, and then I felt that same somebody take me from the tree more dead than alive."

"Where are your brothers and sisters?" asked Sweetest Susan.

"Well, you know how it is in the woods and fields; it is everybody for himself, and everything for itself. Once out of the nest, you must look out for yourself. As for my brothers and sisters, I would n't know them, if I were to see them, and they would n't know me. Sometimes I see my mother, and she always has a hickory nut or a sweet acorn to give me; but as for the rest, I know nothing about them. It is very comfortable here, where you have somebody to clean out the hickory nuts for you, and I suppose I'll never see any of my kind any more. A little more water, if you please — just a drop. Thank you!

"SHE LEANED FORWARD AND LOOKED AT ME"

Now, if you'll put me in a nice soft place I'd like to take a nap."

But before Flit could get any sleep, the children felt in duty bound to show him to their mother and to their grandfather. The White-Haired Master, who never allowed any one to kill or pursue the gray squirrels on his place, took the liveliest interest in Flit. He carried him to the library, sent for some ginned cotton, and made him a nest behind some books on the top shelf, which was not too high for the children to climb to; and there, for many a long day, he made his home.

The library was in a room that had not been originally built for holding books, and the shelves were built against a window, the back of them being boxed in at that point. Flit soon discovered that there was a broken pane behind this boxing, which gave him an easy way of going out and coming in. He went out and in to so much purpose that he soon brought a wife home, and before the summer was over, he had a very interesting family composed of his wife and four plump children, — the wonder and delight of Sweetest Susan, and indeed of all who saw them.

Mrs. Flit was shy at first and insisted on scrambling out in great haste when Buster John or Sweetest Susan came to see the little ones, but she soon grew accustomed to these visits. The four young ones were as tame as kittens from the first, and remained so; and it was sometimes amusing to see them swoop down from the top shelf to the head of some unsuspecting visitor who had been carried to the library, where the White-Haired Master transacted all his business. Sometimes the wives of the neighboring farmers, who called on business, were purposely asked into the library by one or the other of the children. They never failed to utter wild screams when they found a wild thing about the size of a big rat running about over their heads and shoulders.

Incidentally, the children learned one interesting fact in natural history from Flit. They had heard, or had read, that squirrels store up nuts for winter use. But when they mentioned this, Flit's surprise was great.

"Why, what nonsense!" he chirped. "In cold weather we find plenty on the ground under the leaves, and in the trees, too. We bury them for use in summer, before the acorns and nuts are ripe, but we don't need them much after the whiskers begin to grow on the roasting ears in the fields. When the weather is very, very cold, we sleep, and nobody gets hungry when asleep."

After so long a time, the voice of Aunt Minervy Ann was heard, calling the children. She had been around to the quarters, saying good-by to the negroes she found there, and sending farewells to those who were absent. Major Tumlin Perdue, her former master, and Miss Vallie, her young mistress, were going to move to town, and town was a great place in Aunt Minervy Ann's imagination. To go there to live was something wonderful; she did n't feel at all certain that any of her old friends would ever see her again, and she said so, shaking her head solemnly.

"You see me now, an' you better look at me good, kaze I dunno when you 'll see me any mo'. When you tell ol' Aunt Minervy Ann Perdue good-by now, it may be fer de las' time. Marse Tumlin an' Miss Vallie gwine, an' I 'm bleeze ter go wid um fer ter keep up de name er de fambly. I dunno nothin' 't all about deze town doin's; dey may wipe me up, er dey may wipe me down, er dey may wipe me off'n de face er de yeth;

but you kin put yo' 'pen'ence in one thing: Ol' Minervy Ann Perdue will be dar whiles de wipin' gwine on. You kin lay your las' thrip on dat."

Having told the negroes good-by in this solemn manner, Aunt Minervy Ann now came to tell the white folks farewell. And first she called for Buster John and Sweetest Susan; but the children would not hear to any good-by so early in the day. They insisted that Aunt Minervy Ann should stay to dinner and tell them a story. She protested, and they insisted. Finally, driven into a corner, she exclaimed: —

"Ef you tell me 'zackly how I cotch dat ar flyin' squir'l, I 'll stay an' tell you a tale 'bout a diamon' mine dat I 'd like might'ly ter happen wid Marse Tumlin, if it had 'a' been a sho 'nuff diamon' mine. But you got ter tell me de fust pop; no guessin'."

"Tell her, brother," said Sweetest Susan.

"Well," remarked Buster John, "two hawks were after the squirrel. He was on a dead pine. One would try to catch him, and then the other. You came along through the field and saw the hawks, and drove them away. Then you saw Flit, and picked him up and carried him home."

Aunt Minervy Ann made a wild gesture of alarm. "Whar my things? Whar my basket? I 'm gwine 'way fum here. I ain't gwine ter stay whar witcherments gwine on in de broad light er day! Gi' me my basket an' lemme go!"

But the children knew she was only pretending. So they clung to her, and insisted on the story.

XIV.

THE DIAMOND MINE.

"I know what you-all want," said Aunt Minervy Ann, with an air of protest. "You want me ter tell one er dem ar creetur tales. But I kin tell you mo' tales 'bout folks dan what I kin 'bout creeturs. I b'lieve de creetur tales, tooby sho; I dunner how anybody kin he'p b'lievin' um, but dey all tell 'bout de time when de creeturs wuz kinder up in de worl' like folks is now. But sence den, look like dey been takin' de wrong kinder doctor truck, bekaze deyer done swunk up so dey hatter hide out. Dey ain't quit talkin', kaze I hear um say dat A'on an' you-all know how ter hol' confabs wid um. But dey ain't nigh what dey useter be. Folks done come in an' tuck der place. I dunno dat anybody er anything is been bettered by de change; but dar dey is, an' here we is, an' we-all an' dem will hatter scuffle 'roun' an' do de best we kin."

"Well, anyhow, you told us one tale the other day, and you 'll have to tell us another to make it even. You know more than one." This was Buster John's argument.

"Please stay to dinner and tell us one, just one. We are going to have crablanders." This was Sweetest Susan's plea.

Aunt Minervy Ann looked at the little girl and laughed. "Honey, you know my weakness mighty well. Crablanders! I ain't seed none in so long dat I dunno what dey look like, much less how dey make um. I know de name, an' 'member de tas'e, but dat 's all."

"Why, they boil sweet potatoes till they are soft, scrape the skin off, mash them, sprinkle sugar on them, and then wrap them in piecrust and put them in the oven to bake," said Sweetest Susan.

"Sho 'nuff sugar, honey?" inquired Aunt Minervy Ann solemnly. "We ain't had no sho 'nuff sugar at our house sence de battlin' start up."

"Yes," replied Sweetest Susan; "real sugar. We have a barrelful."

"A whole bairlful! Run git de key er de

sto'house an' lemme kneel down by dat bairl an' hug it."

The children laughed, and Sweetest Susan pretended to be going after the keys, but Aunt Minervy Ann detained her. "Don't do dat, honey. Miss Rachel'd think dat ol' Aunt Minervy Ann Perdue come yer fer ter say 'howdy' ter de vittles, stidder sayin' 'good-by' ter de folks."

She paused and looked at the children seriously. "I'll stay sence I hear you say 'dinner,' kaze we don't have too many dinners at our house, an' dem we does have ain't gwine give nobody de dyspepshy. Whar Miss Rachel? I got sump'n I wanter tell her, an' den, atter dinner, I'll tell you a tale, an' den I'll take my foot in my han' an' go on 'bout my business — an' it'll be a long time more 'fo' you see ol' Minervy Ann Perdue."

The children's mother was in her room sewing, and thither they piloted Aunt Minervy Ann. Then they went to amuse themselves the best they could until after dinner. What Aunt Minervy Ann had to tell their mother must have been very funny, for presently they heard her laughing so loudly that they looked at each other and laughed, too, in pure sympathy. For a very long time they had not heard their mother laugh so heartily and so loud, and it gave them pleasure to hear her now.

After a while — a very long while it seemed to the children — the tinkling bell announced dinner, and after that meal was over they waited patiently for Aunt Minervy Ann, who was having her dinner in the kitchen, where she paid Jemimy the highest of compliments by eating a great deal of everything that came to hand. "'T ain't de yappetite, chile; it 's de cookin'. I useter b'lieve dat I could do sump'n wid de pots an' ovens myse'f, but you young folks done got clean ahead er we ol' ones. I hate ter say it, but de trufe mought ez well be tol', speshually when it can't be hid."

This was the sort of flattery Jemimy appreciated, and she piled Aunt Minervy Ann's plate high with the best the kitchen afforded. Then when the guest had finished, Jemimy pressed her to have something else, and declared that Aunt Minervy Ann had been "mincin' an' not eatin'."

Finally, Aunt Minervy Ann, having swallowed as much as she could, announced her intention of hunting for the children; but she did n't have to hunt at all, for they were outside the kitchen door. They would have been inside but for the fact that they had been warned that they must not watch other people while they were eating, neither at the table in the dining room nor anywhere else.

Aunt Minervy Ann wiped her mouth with the back of her hand and laughed when she saw them.

"You-all is de outdoin'est white chillun I ever laid eyes on. You des grab holt er folks an' wring tales out'n um des like dey wring chicken heads off. How you know I got any tale ter tell? I boun' you 'd be sorry fer yo'se'f ef I wuz ter start in an' make up a tale."

Nevertheless, in spite of these protests, Aunt Minervy Ann went around to the front veranda, saying, "I 'll be dat fur on my way home, anyhow," and the children followed her. Once there, she seated herself on the steps, and Buster John, Sweetest Susan, and Drusilla grouped themselves about her. There was so much formality in this that Aunt Minervy Ann laughed and protested once more.

"I declar' ter gracious!" she cried, "you-all

look so solemn an' pious dat it make my head feel empty. You set up here so starchified, des like dey does in church 'fo' de fust song, dat ef my head had been full er tales dey would n't be na'er one in it now. Why, you make me feel like I did de day Brer John Henry Jerding call on me at de 'spe'unce meetin'. He say, 'Sister Puddew,'" —Aunt Minervy Ann was a wonderful mimic, and she rolled her eyes and closed them slowly and flung her head back—"'Sister Puddew, what is de state er your soul? Is you still walkin' in de er—de er—narrer paff?' Dey wuz a whole passul er niggers dar, men an' wimmin, an' some er de wimmin had up an' spoke, an' one un um spoke so loud dat she fell down an' had ter be toted out. Not ter be outdone by um, I riz an' try ter say sump'n nice, but my han's gun ter trimble, an' my knees ter shake, an' my tongue got up in de roof er my mouf clean out'n my reach. Well, ef you-all had been livin' close ter we-all, you 'd know ol' Aunt Minervy Ann lots better 'n you does. When I foun' I can't say what I wanter say, my dander riz. I say, 'Sister Puddew, ez you call 'er, is walkin' right whar she wanter walk an' nowhar else, an' she 's a doin' lots better 'n some er dem what come yer speshually fer ter have fits.'

"Brer John Henry drawed in his breff an' fetch'd a long groan. I 'low, 'Ef youer fetchin' dat groan at me, des walk outer dat door dar, an' I 'll gi' you sump'n ter groan fer, an' you won't stop groanin' nudder twel long atter de doctor git holt er you. Ef you wanter show off, I 'll he'p you. I 'm a mighty han' at he'pin' folks, an' I 'll fix you so folks can see you ez you is.'"

The truth is, Aunt Minervy Ann was talking to get rid of the embarrassment which had seized her. And when the children laughed heartily at her description of the "experience meeting," she felt better.

"Now, den," she said, "I sorter feel like I wuz at home. You-all sot down here and look at me so hard dat it tuck my breff 'way. An' right now I dunno what I come 'roun' here fer."

"Why, you were to tell us a tale, Aunt Minervy Ann," Sweetest Susan declared.

"What I wanter know," remarked Aunt Minervy Ann, "is why you come ter me ter tell a tale, when dey 's so many tale-tellers on de place? What de matter wid dat gal dar?" pointing to

Drusilla. "She got a monst'ous nice mammy; how come she can't tell no tale?" As nobody said anything, Aunt Minervy Ann went on: "What kinder tale you want? Which tale mus' I tell you?"

"Why, if I knew which tale I wanted you to tell, I could tell it myself," said Buster John. "Don't you know any more tales about Brother Rabbit and Brother Fox?"

"Look like you'd 'a' done got your fill er dem kinder tales by dis time," suggested Aunt Minervy Ann. "I don't git tired un um myse'f kaze in der gwines on an' in der windin's up, dem tales tetches folks whar dey live at. Dey does, des ez sho ez youer settin' dar. I had one in my head ter day, an' I come mighty nigh tellin' it to Marse Tumlin, kaze I hear 'im say he gwine in pardnership wid dat ar John Jeems Hightower, which he say he done fin' a gol' mine on his place. Ter hear dat man, you'd think all he had ter do wuz to go out in his back yard an' git a bairlful er pyo gol' wid no mo' trouble dan shovelin' it up an' shovelin' it in. Dat de way he talk, an' when I hear dat, de tale 'bout ol' Brer Fox diamon' mine pop in my head. But I speck you-all done hear 'bout dat mo' times dan you got fingers an' toes."

But the children protested that they had never heard of Brother Fox's diamond mine.

"It seem like dat times wuz mighty hard wid de creeturs, harder dan what dey is wid us right now," remarked Aunt Minervy Ann by way of preface, "an' de creeturs had ter scuffle 'roun' fer ter git vittles ter eat an' cloze ter w'ar. 'T wuz long 'bout de days when Brer Rabbit nabbed Brer Fox's goobers. Fust dey wuz a long dry drout', an' den a long wet rain, dat fresh'd de rivers an' de creeks an' de branches out'n de banks, an' washed up all de craps. Dey wuz mo' swimmin' dan wadin', and mo' wadin' dan walkin' 'bout dat time, an' when de water runn'd off, times wuz des a leetle bit harder dan what dey wuz when de drout' wuz on.

"You-all may n't b'lieve it, but hard times will change habits. Let folks have plenty ter eat, and 'nuff cloze to w'ar, an' dey 'll go on behavin' better an' better; but stint um, an' dey 'll go on behavin' wuss an' wuss. Now dat 's de plain, naked trufe, an' you 'll fin' it out when you git big 'nuff fer ter take notice er all de gwines on you see 'roun' you. Well, 't wuz endurin' deze hard times I 'm tellin' you 'bout dat de creeturs 'gun ter hunt one an'er down. Up ter dem times dey went on an' plant der craps an' work um an' house um des like folks does now. Dey had der corn patches an' der goober patches an' der tater patches an' der peach orchards, an' dey had der barbecues an' dinners, an' ol' Miss Meadows an' de gals wuz dar fer ter have quiltin' bees, an' dey had der log rollin's and sech like.

"But when times got hard, an' den got wuss stidder gittin' better, dey drap der work, kaze 't wan't no use ter work, an' den dey tuck ter stealin', an' bimeby here dey wuz clawin' and chawin' one an'er; de big ones eatin' de little ones, an' de little ones eatin' de littlest, up and down thoo de woods; an' fum dat time on dey wuz wil'. Dey quit war'n cloze, an' ha'r grow'd on um, an' atter dey 'd had blood, bread did n't tas'e good no mo'.

"Yit de time I 'm gwine ter tell you 'bout wuz when times wuz gittin' wusser, but had n't come ter de wuss. De creeturs wuz scufflin' an' scramblin' fer sump'n ter eat, an' none 'cept de biggest had 'gun ter claw an' chaw one an'er. 'Fo' dem hard times dey had been a heap er talk 'bout a diamon' mine in dem parts, an' all dat talk had been handed down for de longest. Brer Wolf had heard his great gran'daddy talkin' 'bout it; Brer Fox gran'daddy know'd sump'n 'bout it, an' Brer Rabbit gran'mammy had 'lowed dat ef she wuz young ez she useter be an' had good use er limbs an' eyes, she could go straight an' put her han' on de place whar de diamon' mine wuz at. All de ol' creeturs talked dat way, an' de ol' ones 'fo' dem, way back yan' when de creeturs wuz bigger dan what hosses is now."

Bigger than horses! The children began to open their eyes, and Sweetest Susan snuggled up to Aunt Minervy Ann with that delightful thrill of make-believe dread that only children can feel. Aunt Minervy Ann knew she had scored a point.

"Yes, la! Bigger dan what hosses is now. Dey 'd set up cross-legged an' run on 'bout dat diamon' mine des like der gran'daddies had done befo' um, an' des like der gran'chillun done atter um. An' when de hard times 'gun ter pinch um, dey start in ter hunt fer dat diamon' mine. Ef dey 'd 'a' worked ez hard ez dey hunted, maybe dey mought er been better off; anyhow dey 'd 'a' felt lots better.

"Brer Wolf went off in de woods by hisse'f, an' Brer Fox by hisse'f, an' Brer Rabbit by hisse'f, an' dat wuz de way wid all de yuthers. Dey don't want nobody ter know ef dey fin' de diamon' mine. Dey hunt an' dey hunt from dawn twel dark, an' when night come dey 'd dream 'bout it. But dey wuz bleeze ter eat, an' some days dey 'd go 'roun' huntin' fer vittles. Brer Rabbit had some acorns dat his ol' 'oman had saved up, an' he foun' some sugar cane dat had been buried in de san' when de freshet come, an' he got 'long tollable well; but he wa'n't none too fat. Brer Wolf wuz thin ez a fence rail, an' Brer Fox wuz so gaunt dat his fambly ain't never got fat down ter dis day.

"Well, one time when de creeturs wuz takin' a day off, Brer Fox he 'low dat he don't b'lieve dey 's any diamon' mine anywhar 'roun' in dat country. But Brer Rabbit say his great-gran'-mammy wuz 'quainted wid dem dat own de mine. Brer Fox he ax what der name wuz. Brer Rabbit 'low dat der name wuz needer mo' ner less dan Mammy-Bammy-Big-Money, an' de way she got her name wuz on 'count er de diamon' mine.

" Brer Wolf laugh and say, ' Dat de trufe, an' what 's mo', Brer Fox would n't know a diamon' fum a pebble less'n it wuz cleaned an' rubbed up.'

" Brer Fox say, ' Don't dey shine like dey got fire in der entrails ? '

" Brer Fox shake his head an' 'low, ' Not less'n deyer cleaned an' rubbed up.'

" Dis make Brer Fox open his eye. He say, ' I been huntin' fer shine-things ; maybe I done fin' de diamon' mine widout knowin' it.'

" ' Maybe you is an' maybe you ain't,' sez Brer Wolf wid a grin, an' Brer Rabbit he laugh fit ter kill.

" Brer Fox he ax what a diamon' look like 'fo' it 's rubbed up an' made shiny.

" ' Des like plain, ev'y-day dirt,' says Brer Wolf, an' Brer Rabbit 'grees wid 'im.

" Well, dey went on huntin'. Dey hunt high an' dey hunt low, an' bimeby dey got so bad off an' so venomous fer vittles dat dey hatter do sump'n 'sides hunt diamon' mines ; an' so, one day, when Brer Wolf see Brer Rabbit gwine 'long thoo de woods, he loped atter 'im. Brer

Rabbit seed 'im comin', an' he cantered on ahead. De faster Brer Wolf come, de faster Brer Rabbit went, an' bimeby Brer Rabbit got in de briar bush whar Brer Wolf can't foller. He got in dar, he did, an' set down an' wipe his face wid bofe han's like you see chillun do. Brer Wolf sot not fur off, an' he was so hongry he fair dribble at de mouf.

"He say, 'Come yer, Brer Rabbit; I wanter see you.'

"Brer Rabbit 'low, 'Look at me, Brer Wolf; I 'm in plain sight. I ain't hidin'.'

"Brer Wolf say, 'I wanter show you sump'n.'

"Brer Rabbit say, 'I ain't got pop-eyes for nothin'. I kin set right here an' see anything you wanter show me ef 't ain't no littler dan a seed-tick.'

"Brer Wolf lick his chops an' say, 'I got sump'n I wanter whisper in yo' year.'

"Brer Rabbit 'low, 'My years ain't big fer nothin'. Do yo' whisper'n from whar you is, Brer Wolf. I kin hear you des ez well, ef not better, dan ef you had my year in yo' mouf.'

"Den Brer Wolf walk 'roun' an' study. Bimeby he look down at de groun' an' sorter scratch in it. Den he jump up in de a'r an' whirl 'roun' an' holler '*Goody-goody*, Brer Rabbit! I so glad I projicked wid you! *Goody-goody!* I done foun' de diamon' mine.' Den he clawed on de groun' wid han's an' foots, an' made de dirt and pebbles fly.

"Brer Rabbit sot dar in de briar bush an' watch Brer Wolf fer ter see what he gwine do nex'. Den he went on combin' his ha'r wid his tongue an' rubbin' his face wid his han's.

"Brer Wolf, wid one eye on Brer Rabbit, kep' up his grabblin' in de dirt. He holler, 'Come on, Brer Rabbit! Deyer here by de bushel. De groun' is fair strowed wid um!'

"Brer Rabbit 'low, 'Nummine 'bout me, Brer Wolf. Ef dey's 'nuff fer bofe, I'll git mine atter you git all you want. Ef dey ain't 'nuff fer bofe, 't ain't no use fer me ter come out dar an' worry you while you workin'.'

"Brer Wolf grabble harder dan ever. He say, 'Oh, come on, Brer Rabbit! Don't be hangin' back dat away!'

"Brer Rabbit 'low, 'I'm gwine home atter a bag. My pockets ain't big 'nuff fer ter hol' all you say you gwine ter gi' me.'

"Brer Wolf say, 'Come look at um, Brer Rabbit, an' choosen de size an' kin' you want.'

"Brer Rabbit 'low, 'I 'd be monst'us ongrateful ef I could n't trust dat ter you, Brer Wolf.'

"Wid dat Brer Rabbit holler, 'Wait fer me, Brer Wolf! Wait fer me!' Den he make a big rustlin' noise in de briar bush like he runnin' thoo um, but he laid his ears back an' drapt on de groun' an' watch Brer Wolf. Time Brer Rabbit made de rustlin' noise, Brer Wolf stopped grabblin', an' run 'roun' de briar patch fer ter see ef he can't head Brer Rabbit off an' ketch 'im.

"When Brer Rabbit see dat, he sot up an' laugh, an' lay down an' laugh, an' roll over an' laugh; an' ez ef dat wan't 'nuff, he drum on de groun' wid his behine foots, an' it soun' des like when you thump on a bedtick wid yo' fingers."

"Then he did n't catch Brother Rabbit?" said Sweetest Susan.

"Who? Him! Not dat day, ner de nex', ner not na'er udder day dat I ever hear tell un. Well, when Brer Wolf got 'roun' de briar patch an' ain't see needer ha'r ner hide er Brer Rabbit, he say ter hisse'f dat Brer Rabbit done gone on home in a hurry, an' he 'll des waylay 'im ez he come back. So he hid in de underbrush an' wait. He wait an' he wait, but Brer Rabbit ain't come back, kaze he was settin' not twenty yards fum Brer Wolf an' watchin' his motions, all de time tryin' ter keep fum laughin' out loud.

"Bimeby, who should come promenadin' 'long but ol' Brer Fox. He wa'n't doin' nothin' in de worl' but huntin' de diamon' mine. Time Brer Wolf see 'im he made a break atter 'im, an' Brer Fox put out ez hard ez he could fer ter keep outer de way. Brer Fox wuz nimble in de feet, but Brer Wolf was hongry, an' so dar 't wuz. Bimeby Brer Fox tuck a tree. Brer Wolf try ter clime up atter 'im, but he done dulled his claws by grabblin' an' dey would n't hold in de bark.

"Den he try de same game on Brer Fox dat he 'd tried on Brer Rabbit. He look at de groun', turn 'roun' a time er two, an' start ter grabblin'. He holler out, 'I mighty glad I played de prank on you, Brer Fox, kaze you lead me right straight ter de diamon' mine; you must 'a' know'd whar 't wuz. Ef you did, I 'm mighty much bleeze ter you, kaze de diamon' mine is right here, an' you shan't lose nothin', Brer Fox.'

"Brer Fox look down at 'im, an' look hard,

but Brer Wolf keep on grabblin'. Brer Fox say, 'Is dey sho 'nuff diamon's, Brer Wolf?'

"Brer Wolf make out he ain't hear 'im, an' keep on a-grabblin'. Bimeby he holler, '*Whoo-ee!* What a big un!' He grabble harder dan ever, an' den he fetched an'er whoop, '*Jiminy cracky!* deze de biggest diamon's I yever is laid eyes on.'

"Brer Fox say, 'Hol' up one un um, Brer Wolf, an' lemme see it.'

"Brer Wolf 'low, 'I ain't got time, Brer Fox; I got ter put in my work 'fo' any er de yuther creeturs come up an' claim der sheer. You ain't he'pin' me none, Brer Fox, but I don't keer 'bout dat. You wuz de 'casion er my findin' um; ef I had n't 'a' been prankin' wid you, an' playin' like I wanter ketch you, I 'd 'a' never foun' dis diamon' mine in de roun' worl'. An' you won't lose nothin' by it, needer.' All de time he wuz talkin', Brer Wolf wuz a-grabblin' an' a-gruntin'.

"Brer Fox say, 'Mus' I come down an' he'p you, Brer Wolf?'

"Brer Wolf 'low, 'Come er stay, des ez you choosen, Brer Fox. You ain't gwine ter lose nothin'.'

"All dat soun' so nice dat Brer Fox start down. He come down de tree a little way, an' den stop; but Brer Wolf ain't payin' no 'tention. He des keep on a-gruntin' an a-grabblin'. Bimeby Brer Fox made a long jump ter git ez fur 'way fum Brer Wolf ez he kin; but time he lit, Brer Wolf had 'im. Dey wuz a kinder scuffle, but, bless yo' soul! Brer Fox time done come.

"Atter while, when Brer Wolf wuz layin' sunnin' hisse'f an' feelin' good, ol' Brer Rabbit come promenadin' 'long. He see Brer Wolf, an' stop. He look all 'roun', an' he see whar de groun' been grabbled up; he look furder, an' he see Brer Fox head layin' on de groun' grinnin'. Den he 'low: —

"'Heyo, Brer Wolf! You must 'a' foun' an'er diamon' mine. Two in one day is big luck — mighty big luck. Brer Fox is sorter swunk up, but what dey is lef' un 'im look mighty happy.'

"Brer Wolf say, '*Oh, go 'way, man! I feel too good!*'"

The story was ended, and so is this book. Aunt Minervy Ann's time was up, and so is mine. Glancing back over its pages, it seems to be but a patchwork of memories and fancies, a confused dream of old times. Perhaps some youngster, tiring of better things, may take it up and follow it to this point, and then close it wondering as to the fate of Billy Biscuit. But his story would make another book, and we cannot have two books in one.